'You've a very pr

Too late, Philippa real

doing. By then, he ha

and let his own mouth briefly explore her lips.

'What do you think you're doing?' she gasped, annoyed—and rather alarmed—by her sudden breathlessness.

'I'd have thought that was fairly obvious. I'm trying to discover how you bewitched Jonathan.'

Dear Reader

Falling in love is exciting...but we all know that it *can* be complicated! For instance, what would you do if the man of your dreams happened to be your father's worst enemy? That's the dilemma faced by Charlotte Lamb's heroine next month in DEADLY RIVALS, the second book in her compelling new series—don't miss it! And you'll find some thrilling love-stories in *this* month's selection, too. We hope you enjoy this one!

The Editor

Joanna Mansell hasn't always wanted to write. It was an idea that popped into her head when she was 'thirty-something', and then wouldn't go away again. It's turned out to be rather addictive, though, and now she has started, she says, she can't stop! When she's not working, she loves reading, gardening, watching films, day-dreaming, and sneaking away from the typewriter on hot, sunny days to go for walks along the seafront.

Recent titles by the same author:

A PERFECT SEDUCTION

DARK TEMPTATION

BY

JOANNA MANSELL

MILLS & BOON

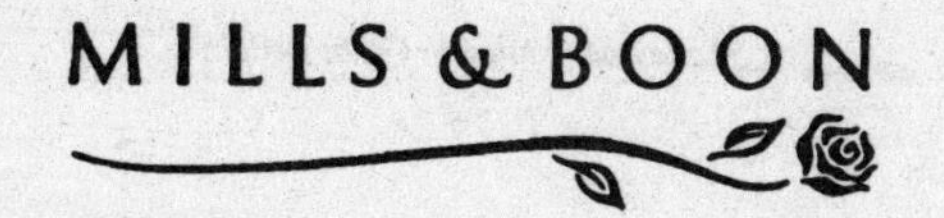

Harlequin Mills & Boon Limited,
Eton House, 18-24 Paradise Road, Richmond, Surrey, TW9 1SR
This edition published by arrangement with Harlequin Enterprises B.V.

ISBN 0 263 78987 X

Set in Times Roman 10 on 12 pt
01-9505-54860 C

Made and printed in Great Britain

CHAPTER ONE

PHILIPPA applied a light covering of special glue to the bright emerald jewel in her hand, and carefully stuck it in her navel. She waited a couple of minutes for the glue to dry, and then tried a couple of experimental rolls and wriggles of her hips.

To her relief, the jewel stayed in place. Last night, it had popped out halfway through her dance routine and rolled across the floor. Very embarrassing!

It wasn't a real emerald, of course, just cut glass, but it still sparkled convincingly as Philippa did a few more stretching exercises, to warm up. Then she stared critically at her reflection in the mirror, finally giving a rueful sigh.

She really wasn't cut out to be a belly-dancer. Oh, she certainly *looked* good, with her long, dark hair, big brown eyes, and the fake tanning lotion that gave her skin a golden glow. And the costume was fine—even if not very authentic! It was the kind of thing that the tourists expected to see, though. Lots of gauzy silk floated around her in bright colours, and more fake jewels were stuck over the thin wisps of material that covered the essential parts of her body. Small silver bells tinkled at her wrists and ankles, and a long veil drifted down her back.

The main problem was that she was too thin. Philippa knew that a belly-dancer ought to be voluptuous, with lots of generous curves. She was built more like a race-horse, she thought wryly, tall and very slender, with not an ounce of spare flesh. And belly-dancing was meant to be erotic, but she just couldn't seem to manage that. She had tried it a couple of times, in private, but had just ended up collapsing into fits of laughter, and had finally given up. Luckily, the audience didn't seem to mind that her belly-dancing was even less authentic than her costume. After a day of exhausting sightseeing, or baking on the beaches in the hot Tunisian sun, most of them just wanted to collapse into the nearest chair, eat a huge meal, and enjoy an undemanding evening of entertainment.

Philippa glanced at her watch. She was due on stage in ten minutes. Just three more nights, she reminded herself, and then she would be returning home to England. This job was only temporary; she was standing in for her friend, Julie, who had had a bad fall and damaged her knee. Julie had recommended Philippa as a stand-in, and the hotel had immediately agreed. It was the height of the holiday season, everyone was frantically busy, and they were relieved that they didn't have to audition a string of hopeful young dancers. They had flown her out at once to replace Julie.

Philippa had been grateful for the work. Although she had auditioned for several summer shows, she hadn't had any success. She was a good dancer, but she just couldn't seem to get the right breaks.

She knew that she was going to have to think about her future very seriously when she got back to England. And it wasn't only her dancing career—or lack of it!—that was giving her a few sleepless nights. Just before flying out to Tunisia, she had impulsively accepted a proposal of marriage. She was already beginning to have doubts, though, and it was something that she was going to have to think about *very* seriously. Not right now, though. She had to concentrate on getting through tonight's performance without any mishaps.

When she reached the stage, her music was already playing. She was billed as 'Roxanne, the world's most exotic bellydancer', which always made her grin. Philippa privately thought that the hotel was lucky the Trades Description Act didn't apply in Tunisia!

It was a relief to give all her attention to her dancing and forget about her personal problems for a while. The stage projected out into the middle of the room, with tables set all round it. Philippa shimmied into the spotlight, and then began her routine. She had to dance on the stage for several minutes, and then move down among the audience, flirting gently with the men, but in a friendly way, so that their wives weren't offended. That was easy. Everyone was on holiday and in a relaxed mood; they knew that this was just entertaining fun and not to be taken seriously.

The lights dimmed, and she had everyone's attention as she rolled and wriggled her hips sinuously. To her relief, the green jewel stayed exactly where she had stuck it, and she moved confidently down from the stage and began to dance between the tables.

She always enjoyed this part of the show; she liked being close to the audience and seeing their reaction to her dancing on their faces. This week, many of the hotel guests were pensioners, here on a special package tour for the over sixties. They were a jolly crowd, and obviously determined to enjoy every moment of their holiday. Last night, Philippa had persuaded some of them to join in the routine, and everyone had roared with laughter as plump, elderly ladies—and a couple of gentlemen!—had put on silk veils and silver bells, and shaken and wiggled enthusiastically to the music.

Tonight, though, she was just going straight through her routine. She danced her way round the room, spinning lithely so that the gauzy silk spun in a rainbow of colours around her body. Slightly breathless, she finished up facing a table in the very far corner of the room.

This table had just one man sitting at it, and he definitely *wasn't* a pensioner. Philippa didn't remember seeing him around the hotel before tonight. If she had, she was sure she would have remembered him. Those dark, brooding good looks stood out a mile! Piercing blue eyes fringed with long, dark lashes, a harshly beautiful mouth, dark hair that swept back from a high, intelligent forehead, and the kind of bone-structure that would make a painter or sculptor weep from pure joy—the man had everything. Even his clothes marked him out from the people around him. All the other hotel guests wore bright, casual holiday outfits, but he was immaculately dressed in a dark suit and crisp white shirt, every inch of cloth fitting him to perfection.

And, most amazing of all, this staggeringly impressive man was looking directly back at her with intense interest!

Philippa felt her stomach flutter with pure excitement. Then, as that blue gaze remained fixed on her, that inner tremor spread right through her, from the roots of her hair to the very tips of her toes.

This was slightly crazy, she warned herself. And she certainly couldn't stand here all evening in a complete daze, just staring back at him. She had to keep on dancing!

She somehow managed to move her feet and half-heartedly swayed her hips, although she knew that she had lost all sense of rhythm. And she still couldn't seem to stop *looking* at him, despite the fact that those blue eyes were the most intimidating she had ever seen.

Then his face changed, and that intense scrutiny suddenly gave way to a dark and quite unmistakable expression of contempt.

It was so unexpected that it made Philippa catch her breath. At the same time, an unpleasant wave of physical shock ran through her. What had she done to make him react like that? Didn't he like the show? She appreciated that this kind of entertainment wasn't to everyone's taste, but no one was forcing him to watch it. He was free to walk out.

He didn't move, though. And the contempt on his face deepened.

She knew that it couldn't be personal: he didn't even know her. So she guessed that it *had* to be the show. That made her a little angry. What right did he have to sneer at something that gave the hotel guests a lot of pleasure? All right, so it wasn't top-line entertainment, but it wasn't meant to be. It was a colourful show for tourists who just wanted to relax for a couple of hours at the end of the day. If he wanted something more highbrow, then he shouldn't have booked into a holiday hotel!

With a touch of defiance, she tossed back her long, dark hair and began to gyrate her hips with new vigour. He didn't like belly-dancing? Well, bad luck. He was about to get some more of it!

The man's brilliant blue gaze raked over her disparagingly as she danced in front of him. To her alarm, Philippa felt herself suddenly going very hot, as if those extraordinary eyes had the power to burn her. Hey, she thought shakily, what was going on here?

She suddenly wanted to back off, to get as far away as she could from this very disturbing stranger. She refused to behave like a coward, though, and she gritted her teeth and danced on, absolutely determined not to run away, not even if she melted right into the floor!

She rolled her stomach muscles energetically, giving the performance of her life. The rest of the audience began to clap and cheer as the tempo got faster and faster, and Philippa sinuously swayed and spun, her feet moving effortlessly in a series of complicated steps. She gave one last defiant roll of her hips, and at the same time shot a bold look at the dark-haired man. How do you like that? she silently challenged him.

Then her mouth dropped open in pure dismay as the green emerald popped out of her navel and bounced across the floor, to land at the man's feet.

Philippa froze. She didn't know what to do. She certainly didn't know what to say!

The man picked up the emerald and then slowly got to his feet. He was tall—*very* tall, she realised, with a gulp. She was over five feet eight, but her head was barely level with his shoulders.

He held the emerald out to her and, very reluctantly, she took it. She saw that her fingers were shaking slightly, and that annoyed her. She hadn't wanted him to know that he could affect her in any way.

Those blue eyes fixed on her scathingly one last time. 'A tawdry little jewel,' he said in a voice as powerful and cold as his face. 'It suits you.'

Then, having delivered that deliberate insult, he turned round and strode off.

Philippa very slowly became aware that the music was still playing; that she was expected to carry on dancing. People were already beginning to murmur because she was just standing there, absolutely transfixed by the man's deliberate and cruel rudeness.

With an enormous effort, she forced herself to move. And to smile. And to dance. All the time, though, her head was whirling. Why had that happened? And who *was* that man?

She went through the last part of her routine mechanically, and was enormously relieved when it was finally over. She hurriedly left the stage, glad to leave behind all those curious eyes staring at her from the audience as everyone wondered exactly what had happened during that unscheduled break in her dance.

Philippa herself didn't understand what had happened. Those eyes! She gave a small shiver as she remembered how they had seemed to see right inside her head, into every secret little corner. She fervently wished that she didn't have to go back on to that stage tonight, but there was still the rest of the show to get through. The hotel hadn't flown her all the way out to Tunisia so that she could belly-dance for a quarter of an hour every night! She also doubled as the magician's assistant, and appeared in the grand finale, singing and dancing with the rest of the small troupe. And during the day she was also kept busy. She organised dance exercise classes for any holiday-makers with enough energy and enthusiasm, and helped to put on impromptu shows to entertain the children staying at the hotel, while their parents took a well-earned break or went sightseeing.

At the moment, though, she had a half-hour break. That gave her plenty of time to whip off her costume, wipe the kohl from her eyes, and put on the embroidered robe and veil she had to wear as 'Yasmin', the magician's assistant, supposedly all the way from the mysterious East.

She had a tiny room at the back of the stage where she kept her costumes and make-up. Usually, she shared it with two sisters who did a juggling and acrobatic act, but tonight was their night off, so she had it to herself for once.

Philippa pushed the door open, glad that there was no one to see the disturbed state she was in. She would have half an hour to get herself together again before she was due back on stage—and she would need every minute of it! Tonight had been odd—*very* odd. Her pulses were still racing, and she could hear that arrogant, insulting voice echoing inside her head.

As soon as she walked into the dressing-room, however, all her senses flared with fresh alarm. She smelt him first of all—a fresh male scent that made her nerve-ends quiver in a way that was quite new to her. Then she saw him, intimidatingly tall, his blue eyes already boring into her as she froze on the spot.

Somehow, she stopped her nerves from flying apart. 'What are you doing here?' she demanded, relieved that her voice wasn't as shaky as her legs. 'Guests aren't allowed backstage; this part of the hotel is private.'

He ignored her question. Instead his gaze flicked over her skimpy costume. 'Get dressed,' he ordered. 'You're leaving.'

'What on earth are you talking about?' she said incredulously. 'I'm not going anywhere. And especially not with you!'

His dark face registered a swift wave of impatience. 'I do have the right girl? You are Philippa Martin?'

'Yes, I am.'

'Then I insist that you return to England with me. We can catch the late evening flight.'

This was getting crazier by the minute. Philippa suddenly decided that she had had enough of it. 'Who *are* you?' she demanded.

'James Haverford, of course,' he said tersely.

Understanding finally washed over Philippa. At the same time, she began to shake all over again. 'James Haverford?' she repeated in a much fainter voice. 'The—the Earl of Sherringborne? Jonathan's uncle?'

Just before flying out to Tunisia, and after a whirlwind romance, she had become engaged to Jonathan Haverford. She had known that Jonathan came from a titled family, of course, but she had never met any of his relatives. There simply hadn't been time. More than once, though, Jonathan had affectionately referred to 'old Uncle James'. Philippa had conjured up a mental picture of a grey-haired old man, rattling round inside his stately home and living in the past. She had certainly not expected the Earl of Sherringborne to be in his late thirties, in superb physical shape, and to have the kind of looks that made her nerve-ends go completely haywire!

James Haverford frowned at her, his mouth setting into a hard line. 'I would have flown out earlier, but I was tied up with urgent business affairs. I've finally seen your act, though, and it's obviously completely inappropriate for Jonathan's future wife. I'm amazed that Jonathan allowed it.'

'Jonathan didn't have any say in the matter,' Philippa said with a fresh surge of pure indignation. 'I run my own life! But he certainly knew about it—and approved. He understood that working would help the time pass more quickly for me while he was away.'

Jonathan was mountain-climbing in the Himalayas. The expedition had been arranged for months before he had even met her, and although he had wanted to cancel it after she had said yes to his proposal of marriage he couldn't pull out without ruining the trip for the three friends he was going with. Since Philippa had already had the offer of the temporary job in Tunisia, she had persuaded him to go ahead with the trip, although it had taken her a long time to convince him that she would be all right on her own for the couple of months that he would be away. Jonathan was the protective type, which Philippa had found rather endearing. Independence was fine, but she had rather guiltily enjoyed having someone to worry about her and wanting to look after her.

But now she was face to face with Jonathan's uncle, the Earl of Sherringborne, and that was a *very* different matter.

Philippa forced herself to stare at him boldly. 'I don't understand how you even know about our engagement. It was meant to be a secret.'

In fact, it had been Jonathan who had suggested that they tell no one for a while. Philippa had expected him to tell his family straight away, and she had been surprised when he had said that he wanted to keep it their private secret. She had briefly wondered if it was because she was just an ordinary person, no title, no inherited wealth, no distinguished family tree that could be traced back for generations, but she had immediately been ashamed of that thought. Jonathan certainly wasn't a snob. Then he had explained that he wanted to wait until he had had a chance to do the whole thing properly. He had proposed on the spur of the moment, in the back of a taxi. When he came back from the Himalayas, he wanted to do it all over again in the traditional way, on one knee and producing an engagement ring with a flourish!

But he had obviously changed his mind about that. Their engagement wasn't their private secret any longer. For some reason, Jonathan had told his uncle all about it. Why? Philippa wondered, with a puzzled frown.

She soon found out.

'Jonathan has never been able to keep any secrets from me,' James Haverford said curtly. 'And it's as well that I found out about it before any real damage is done.'

'Damage?' she said indignantly. 'What on earth are you talking about?'

'You're not naïve,' he said in a hard voice. His powerful blue gaze slid over her assessingly. 'In fact, you seem the kind of girl who understands very well how the world works.' Philippa was quite sure that he had meant that insultingly, but before she could challenge him on it he went on, 'Once the Press find out that the nephew of the Earl of Sherringborne is engaged to a belly-dancer they'll run the lurid kind of stories for which they're famous—or, rather, infamous. I intend to run a damage-limitation exercise. Once you're installed at Sherringborne Manor, I'll have control over any further publicity. When the Press are starved of publicity photographs and personal interviews, they tend to lose interest fairly quickly.'

'Now wait just a minute,' Philippa said fiercely. 'Are you suggesting that I come and stay at Sherringborne Manor, to hide from the Press?'

'I'm not suggesting anything. I'm telling you how I intend to handle this situation. You'll stay at Sherringborne until Jonathan returns home, when there will be a quiet announcement of your engagement. Neither of you will have any direct contact with the Press.

We'll issue an official photograph, and I'll handle any subsequent publicity.'

Philippa couldn't believe she was hearing this. Who did this man think he was, powering his way into her life and coolly announcing that he intended to take it over?

'Let's get one thing straight *right now*,' she said heatedly. 'I am *not* coming back to England with you. I am *not* going to stay at Sherringborne Manor. And I'm most certainly not going to let you interfere in something that's private between me and Jonathan!'

'If you're marrying into the Haverford family, then your business becomes my business,' he said brutally. 'Unless you understand that from the very beginning, you're heading for a great deal of trouble.'

But she refused to let him intimidate her. 'Even if I did want to go with you to England—which I don't!—I'm not free to leave,' she reminded him fiercely. 'I'm under contract to the hotel. I'm going to be working here until the end of this week.'

'Contracts can be broken,' he said at once. 'I can arrange it.'

Oh, yes, she was sure that he could! She was absolutely certain that he was a man who could arrange anything.

'I've no intention of breaking my contract,' she told him vehemently. 'In this business, you can quickly get a bad reputation by doing that kind of thing.'

'I assume that you're talking about your dancing career?' His tone was so completely disparaging that Philippa's brown eyes immediately blazed.

'Yes, I mean my career! Believe it or not, it's important to me.'

'I'm sure that belly-dancing in a holiday hotel is the very peak of every dancer's ambition.'

There was no sarcasm in his voice, which she could perhaps have handled. Instead there was just the cool insinuation that she wasn't capable of anything better.

'I suppose that, when Jonathan told you I was a dancer, you expected a prima ballerina?' she retorted. 'Or the star of a modern dance company? Well, sorry to disappoint you,' she went on, and her own voice was sarcastic now, 'but I expect it'll be quite a novelty for the Haverfords to have a belly-dancer in the family!'

James Haverford's intense blue gaze met hers and easily held it. 'You and Jonathan are only engaged,' he said softly. 'Not married.'

She didn't know how he had done it—he hadn't even raised his voice—but he had managed to make that simple statement sound like a threat.

But Philippa didn't intend to let anyone threaten her, not even the Earl of Sherringborne.

'But we will be married,' she said defiantly, completely ignoring the fact that she already had doubts about her whirlwind engagement. Right now, for some reason that she didn't even understand, standing up to this man seemed more important than anything else.

James Haverford's face altered—a darkness swept over it, making Philippa suddenly shiver in response. He looked so grim, so formidable!

'Jonathan is younger than you,' he pointed out tersely. 'He's only just twenty years old.'

'And I'm twenty-four. That's not exactly ancient! If it were the other way round, everyone would think the age-gap was perfect.'

'Women in their early twenties are often more mature than men.' His piercing gaze raked over her again, and it took all of Philippa's will-power to stop herself instinctively shrinking back from that sweeping scrutiny. 'I think that you are probably very mature—and experienced—for your age,' he said in a hard tone.

She decided that was the very last insult she intended to take from him.

'Please leave my dressing-room, Lord Sherringborne,' she said icily. 'I don't want to talk to you any more, and I think that I've already made it perfectly plain that I've no intention of returning to England with you.'

He glanced at his watch. 'It's already too late to catch the evening flight. We'll discuss this again in the morning.'

'No, we will not!' Philippa told him furiously. 'You don't seem to be getting the message, so I'll say it once more in words that even you'll be able to understand. This subject is closed!'

A dark anger glowed in his eyes, as if he wasn't used to having his orders disobeyed by a mere girl. 'It most certainly isn't,' he said tersely. 'We will talk about this again very soon. In fact, if you insist on going ahead with your marriage to my nephew, then I shall have a great deal to say to you,' he warned grimly.

'I don't want to hear it!'

The glow in his eyes intensified to a dangerous level. 'Don't push me, Miss Martin. Jonathan is friendly, easygoing and good-tempered. I am not. You would do well to remember that.'

With that threat delivered, the Earl of Sherringborne fixed the full force of that punitive stare on her for several more seconds before finally turning round and striding from the room.

* * *

Philippa somehow got through the rest of the evening, forcing herself to go back on stage and go through her routines automatically. Then she thankfully escaped up to her tiny bedroom. Even after she had locked the door, though, she couldn't make herself relax completely. Part of her still half expected James Haverford to force the door open and come striding through, his powerful gaze pinning her down while he delivered some more deliberate insults.

'He might be Jonathan's uncle, but I'm always going to hate that man!' she told herself fiercely as she pulled off her clothes and wriggled into her nightshirt. 'And I will *not* go and stay at his house.'

She climbed into bed, but then couldn't sleep. She felt agitated and slightly feverish; every time she closed her eyes she could see that dark, arrogant face staring at her. In the end, she groaned out loud in frustration and thumped the pillows.

'James Haverford is not going to stop me getting a good night's sleep,' she told herself defiantly. She closed her eyes, made a huge effort to blot the image of his face from her mind, and told herself it was only the sultriness of the night that was making her feel so hot and restless.

Through sheer determination, she finally fell asleep. She had some funny, mixed-up dreams, though, which she quickly tried to forget when she woke up the next morning.

The sun was shining brilliantly outside her window, and the temperature was steadily climbing. Philippa had a free morning, and decided she didn't want to stay in the hotel. She might run into the Earl of Sherringborne again, and that would certainly ruin her day!

She was confident that she could avoid him for the next few hours. With luck, he would grow tired of looking for her, decide she simply wasn't worth the effort, and go back home.

That sounded fine, in theory. Philippa had the deep conviction, though, that James Haverford never gave up once he had embarked on a certain course of action.

Why, oh, *why* had Jonathan had to blurt the news of their engagement to his uncle? It would only make everything much more difficult if she finally decided that she wanted to call it off. Jonathan would have to face the humiliation of everyone in his family knowing that he had been jilted.

And was she thinking of calling it off? Philippa wondered anxiously. She really didn't know. She adored Jonathan, but she wasn't quite certain if that was the same as loving him. The problem was, she didn't have much experience in these matters. She knew that she tended to keep other people at arm's length, even her friends. She supposed it was because of her isolated childhood, being the only child of elderly parents who had been very over-protective, trying to shield her from the world but only succeeding in shutting her away from it.

Then Jonathan had burst into her life. Philippa's face relaxed into a soft smile as she thought about him. They had only known each other for such a short time, but she had been quite bowled over by his friendliness, his charm, his ability to laugh at life and turn even a dull evening into a few hours of sheer fun. And he was good-looking, too, although not in the least like his dark, brooding uncle. Jonathan was blond-haired and blue-eyed, one of life's golden people. Philippa had loved being with him, and been quite astonished when he had proposed to her.

'You must say yes,' he had said persuasively. 'You don't want me to be unhappy and lovesick while I'm climbing in the Himalayas, do you? If I'm pining for you all the time, I might lose my concentration and fall off the mountain!'

And Philippa, laughing, full of champagne, and dazzled by all the attention he had lavished on her since they had met, had found herself saying yes.

They should have given each other more time, of course. They probably would have if Jonathan hadn't been going away. Everything had suddenly seemed very urgent, as if they needed to make some kind of commitment, to stop them drifting apart during his absence.

Once he had gone, Philippa had thought she would have a breathing-space, to try and sort out her true feelings. But there was the problem—the very *big* problem—of the Earl of Sherringborne.

Well, there was something she could do about that, Philippa decided. Keep out of his way!

She slipped out of the hotel by one of the back entrances. She intended to spend the morning wandering around the bazaar. Before she flew back home at the end of the week, she wanted to buy a couple of small presents for friends, and a thank-you gift for Mrs Mackie, her neighbour, who was keeping an eye on her flat while she was away.

There were no family presents to buy. Philippa's parents had died when she was in her late teens. Although she had so often felt completely stifled by their over-protectiveness, that hadn't stopped her from missing them very badly. And although their deaths had meant that the independence she had fought for for so long had suddenly been forced on her, she'd soon realised that it had a downside. Because she had no brothers or sisters, or close relations, she sometimes felt a frightening sense of loneliness.

Perhaps that was why she had so readily agreed to Jonathan's proposal. She was beginning to realise that independence was fine, but it was no substitute for a family. She wanted to *belong* somewhere, and she hoped that Jonathan's family would eventually accept her as one of them.

James Haverford had certainly dashed those hopes, though. He was never going to accept her!

Philippa shook off the slight sense of depression that was beginning to settle over her, and hurried along the narrow road that led to the bazaar.

The sun was blisteringly hot, glaring down out of a brilliant blue sky and reflecting off the white walls of the houses. The road was crowded with people, traffic, donkeys and even the occasional camel, and the bazaar, when she finally reached it, was even more packed. Tourists flocked here from the hotels, hoping to find a bargain. Gold, copper and silver glinted everywhere, there were fragrant smells from the spices and perfumes, and other, more earthy odours from the meat, fish and cheese stalls. Patterned rugs and bright bolts of cloth were stacked precariously high, and all around her Philippa could hear endless haggling over prices.

She couldn't afford anything too expensive, but some of the small copper pots were very attractive and just about within her budget, if she could haggle the prices down a bit. She picked a couple out and prepared to bargain for them. Before she had a chance to say a word, however, a hand descended on her shoulder and gripped it so hard that she yelped out loud in surprise.

'You've been deliberately avoiding me,' said the Earl of Sherringborne in a grim voice.

'I have not!' Philippa lied at once, spinning round to face him. 'I had some shopping to do. I don't have to ask your permission before I leave the hotel!' she finished defiantly, ignoring the hard, heavy thumping of her heart.

'You knew that I wanted to talk to you this morning——'

'Do you like the pots?' the stallholder interrupted anxiously, not wanting to lose a potential sale. 'They're very beautiful—and very reasonable.'

James whipped the pots out of her hand and set them back on the stall. 'She doesn't want them,' he said tersely. Then, still gripping her tightly, he marched her away, out of the bazaar.

'What do you think you're doing?' she demanded breathlessly as she found herself being forced along at breakneck speed.

'Taking you somewhere we can have a private conversation.'

'I don't want to talk to you!'

'Don't be childish,' James said dismissively. At the same time, he steered her down a quiet, narrow alleyway, filled with glaring sunlight that brought her skin out in a flush of heat. Or was it the man still holding on to her who was doing that? she suddenly wondered with a quick surge of unease. She had never met anyone in the least like him before, someone who knew exactly what he wanted and went after it in a frighteningly single-minded fashion.

His brilliant blue eyes were fixed on her now, but they were carefully guarded; it was impossible to read what lay behind them. That was something else that bothered

Philippa. She would have felt a lot safer if she could have guessed what this man was thinking.

Safer? she repeated to herself silently, with a small jolt of alarm. Did she feel threatened by him?

Yes, she did, she decided. But not because he had her cornered in a quiet alleyway. After all, there were crowds of people in the bustling bazaar, just a few yards away. She only had to shout, and someone would come. What he threatened was her peace of mind. She was quite certain that no one who crossed swords with James Haverford walked away unscathed!

She forced herself to glare at him as fiercely as she could. She didn't intend to let him know that he had any effect on her at all—except, perhaps, to irritate the hell out of her.

'Well?' she said, amazed at how bold and challenging her voice sounded. 'What do you want to talk about?'

'I want to know the date of your arrival at Sherringborne Manor.'

Philippa gave an exaggerated sigh. 'I told you last night that I've no intention of staying at your house.'

His blue eyes suddenly narrowed. 'Is there some reason why you're afraid to visit Jonathan's home?'

'I'm not afraid of anything!' Philippa said hotly at once. 'But my mind's made up. When I leave Tunisia, I'm going back to my own flat.'

He took a step back. 'Selfish as well as wilful,' he said in disgust. 'If your marriage to Jonathan ever takes place, then I rate its chances of success as almost non-existent.'

'What do you mean, if it ever takes place?' she demanded, ruffled all over again by this man's infuriating attitude.

James's eyes grew hard. 'It would be difficult to find anyone who would be a more unsuitable match for my nephew.'

'Why?' she said angrily. 'Because I've got a mind of my own, and I won't meekly fall in with all these plans you've made for me? Or is it because I'm a dancer? Just a very ordinary person who has to earn a salary, no one special? That's it, isn't it?' she rushed on. 'You think I'm not good enough for Jonathan; I'm not the right type to marry into a titled family. He can trace his ancestors back for generations—I bet that paintings of them are hanging on all the walls, while all my parents had were a few faded photographs of their grandparents!'

'You sound like the one with all the prejudices,' James said tautly. 'I judged you unsuitable because you don't seem to give a damn for Jonathan's feelings.'

'Of course I do! He's the nicest person I've ever met; I wouldn't do *anything* to hurt him.'

'And what the hell do you think it's going to do to him if the Press find out about your engagement and descend on you here, at the hotel, to take photos of you half naked, dancing in front of ogling groups of tourists?' he said scathingly.

'The Press won't find out unless someone tells them.' Her brown eyes suddenly widened. 'Is that it?' she demanded fiercely. 'Are you threatening me with Press exposure if I won't do what you say?'

'I don't need to resort to that kind of cheap trick,' he said in disgust. 'But rumours spread quickly, and some of Jonathan's friends might not be very discreet.'

'Jonathan's friends don't know about the engagement,' she retorted, but there wasn't quite as much conviction in her voice as she had intended. After all, Jonathan had said he wasn't going to tell *anyone*, but he had certainly told his uncle. And if the Press did find out about it, the whole situation could easily deteriorate into a nightmare of publicity. The gossip columnists would certainly have a field day!

'Look,' she said at last, 'I certainly want to do what's best for Jonathan. I'll think about it and let you know my decision later.'

His finger instantly hooked under her chin, forcing her face up so that it was only inches away from his own powerful features.

'Just make sure that it's the right decision,' James warned, his brilliant blue eyes boring into hers until their intensity seemed to burn like a fire.

CHAPTER TWO

PHILIPPA literally sagged with relief when James finally wheeled round and strode away from her. She had never met anyone who had such a disastrous effect on her nervous system!

She hurried back to the hotel, and spent the afternoon helping to entertain the handful of children staying there this week. It was a part of her job that she always enjoyed, and the time passed quickly. She soon became involved in the games and improvised show that she and a couple of others from the entertainment staff put together, and almost managed to forget about James Haverford for a couple of hours. Almost, but not quite. She was quite sure that he was a man it would be impossible to forget completely, in *any* circumstances.

When the show was finally over and the children had been returned to their parents, Alan, one of the other entertainers, came over to her.

'Don't forget it's barbecue night tonight,' he reminded her.

Philippa had temporarily forgotten, and she gave a small groan. 'I hate dancing on the beach,' she said with some feeling. 'The sand's so soft that I can't move properly and I keep sinking into it. Instead of belly-dancing, I end up shuffling around like an old woman!'

Alan grinned. 'I can't imagine you ever looking old. And the guests love the barbecue; they think it's very romantic eating on the beach under the stars.'

'Well, it'll be my last one,' she said with some regret. 'Julie's fully recovered now; she'll be back next week.'

'We'll miss you,' said Alan. 'You've fitted in really well. It's a shame you can't stay on.'

'I don't think the hotel needs two belly-dancers,' she said, with a grin. Then she glanced at her watch. 'I'm going to grab something to eat. See you tonight at the barbecue.'

Later on, as the great golden orb of the sun began to drift down towards the horizon, Philippa began to get herself ready for the barbecue. As soon as the sun disappeared, a velvet darkness would softly drift over the hotel's private beach and the barbecue fires would be lit.

Tonight, she was going to be wearing a costume of thin silk veils which drifted around her in changing shades of green. The costume was trimmed with gold, so that it would glitter as it caught and reflected the light from the fires that would be burning on the beach. From her small window she could see that the hotel guests were already beginning to make their way down through the palm trees to the long stretch of sand beyond. Very soon she would have to go down and join them. She was going to dance while they ate, hopefully adding some colour to what was billed by the hotel as a 'Tunisian evening under the stars'.

Philippa professionally painted her eyes with kohl, which made them look absolutely enormous. Gold already sparkled on her eyelids, and her lips were coloured brightly. She gave a small grimace when she had finished applying the make-up. Usually she wore very little, and then only in soft, subtle colours. On the darkened beach, though, this exaggerated effect would look just fine.

She could see the flames from the barbecue already beginning to flicker. It was time to go down and start the show. She knew that it was going to be a very long evening because, once she and the rest of the small troupe of entertainers had finished their routines, they were expected to mingle with the guests. In particular, they had to look after anyone on their own. The hotel wanted everyone to enjoy the evening and not feel left out because they didn't have a partner.

As Philippa left the hotel and walked across the sand, she had to admit that it *was* a romantic setting. The tall, waving palms were etched blackly against the starlit sky, the waves murmured softly in the background, lanterns hung from poles set into the ground, covering the beach with small, coloured pools of light, and the smell of food was beginning to waft enticingly on the air as the kitchen staff got the barbecue under way.

To her relief, the evening went well, and the entertainment was obviously enjoyed by everyone. Once the show was over, she and the rest of the entertainment staff went to join the guests. Philippa had been assigned to Mr Roberts, a middle-aged divorced man who was on holiday on his own. To begin with, it wasn't a problem; they talked together and later on danced. But he had been drinking steadily all evening, and his conversation gradually became more suggestive, he clutched her much too tightly when they danced, and his hands began to wander.

The hotel laid down very firm guidelines about this kind of situation. In no circumstances whatsoever was a member of staff allowed to be rude to a guest. If things became difficult, the person involved was simply to walk away. The incident would then be reported to one of the managers, who would deal with it.

Philippa didn't want Mr Roberts to be involved in any kind of trouble; she understood that he was simply lonely, a long way from home, and rather drunk. She certainly didn't intend to be groped all evening, though! She made an excuse about a sudden bad headache, then slipped quietly away from the main group, disappearing into the shadows at the far end of the beach.

She gave a small sigh of relief and congratulated herself on handling the situation diplomatically. She guessed that Mr Roberts would be very apologetic in the morning when he sobered up and remembered how he had behaved. The luminous hands of her watch told her it was well past midnight, and she decided to make her way back to the hotel. She had more than fulfilled her duties for the night!

When she turned to leave, though, a tall, powerful figure stepped out from behind the palm trees that fringed the beach, and blocked her path. Then an already familiar voice spoke, setting all of her nerves completely on edge.

'I'm still waiting for your decision,' James Haverford said in a dark tone.

Philippa was so completely unnerved by his sudden appearance that for a few seconds she couldn't say anything at all. Then she finally managed to find her voice and nervousness made her snap at him edgily.

'How long have you been standing there spying on me?'

He came closer, and she could see the dangerous glow in his eyes. 'Long enough to see that you spread your favours around fairly freely.'

She was glad that it was dark enough to hide the redness that spread right across her face. He had seen her with Mr Roberts—and completely misunderstood the situation!

'I was simply being nice to him,' she said defensively.

'And how many other guests have you been "nice" to since you've been here?' he enquired scathingly.

'You've got it all wrong——'

'I don't think so,' he cut in. He was standing just a few feet away now, and Philippa found herself wishing that there were much more distance between them—like a few hundred miles!

'Personally, I don't give a damn how many men you string along. But if you hurt Jonathan in any way...' he threatened.

'I was *told* to be friendly to Mr Roberts! It's hotel policy; we have to look after guests who are on their own.'

'And you obey because you're a good little employee,' James said cynically.

'I certainly don't want to lose my job.'

'Why not? You've already got a new meal ticket. You've hooked Jonathan.'

That fresh burst of cynicism left her almost speechless. And very angry!

'How dare you say something like that?' she managed to get out at last.

'Oh, very easily, Miss Martin,' he said softly. 'You see, I understand little girls like you. I understand them very well.'

'Don't talk to me like that,' Philippa said fiercely. 'I'm not a little girl. I'm an adult.'

'Then I want to hear that you've made an adult decision about coming to Sherringborne,' James retaliated at once.

Very clever, she thought with some bitterness. He had very neatly trapped her.

'Or were you lying when you said that you wouldn't do anything to hurt Jonathan?' he added, driving home his point. 'Because it will certainly hurt him if he gets caught up in any unsavoury publicity.'

Philippa was silent for a long while. She didn't want to stay under the same roof as James Haverford, not even for one night. He so obviously thought that she was an opportunist, a second-rate dancer and a third-rate human being!

But she certainly didn't want to cause any problems for Jonathan. And staying at his home, meeting the rest of his family might help her to decide whether she really wanted to go through with this engagement. She was increasingly full of doubts that she really needed to resolve in her own mind.

'I finish working here on Sunday,' she told James at last, very reluctantly. 'I'm flying back to England on Monday morning. I could come down to Sherringborne in the afternoon.'

'I'll send a car to pick you up at the airport and bring you directly to the house.'

'I can find my own way there,' she said at once.

His black eyebrows gently rose. 'You've got your own car?'

'Well—no,' she admitted. She couldn't afford one.

'Then you'll need transport. The nearest station is a few miles away, and no buses run near Sherringborne Manor.'

'I'll take a taxi,' Philippa told him rashly. Inwardly, though, she flinched. The train and taxi fares would make a big hole in her very small savings. She was quite determined, however, that this man wasn't going to arrange any part of her life for her.

But James ignored that remark. 'My driver will be waiting for you when your flight lands,' he informed her.

She looked at him in pure exasperation. Hadn't he been listening to a single word she had said? It really was amazing that Jonathan actually seemed to *like* this infuriating man who was his uncle.

'I don't want a driver,' she said very clearly, so that he couldn't possibly pretend that he hadn't heard her. 'I don't even want to go directly to Sherringborne Manor. I need to go back to my own flat first, to collect some clothes and personal belongings.'

'That isn't a problem. My driver will make a detour.'

'You're *still* not listening,' she said through clenched teeth, fighting furiously hard to hold on to her temper. 'I'll make my own travelling arrangements, and I'll come to Sherringborne Manor when I'm ready!'

James's own eyes suddenly narrowed warningly. 'You're determined to make this as difficult as possible, aren't you?'

'I'm not being difficult! But I'm used to running my own life. I don't like other people stepping in and just taking over.'

'Miss Martin, I am not interested in taking over your life,' he said tersely. 'But I am getting very tired of these endless arguments. It was extremely inconvenient for me to come here, and you've gone out of your way to make the situation even more difficult. But now that I am here I intend to get this situation settled to my own satisfaction.'

'Well, it *is* settled,' she retorted. 'I'm going to come to the Manor—but in my own time. That should be good enough for you.'

'It isn't,' he said flatly.

'Oh, you're impossible! What makes you think you've got the right to dictate to me? But I suppose your family has been trampling all over people for centuries,' Philippa said scornfully. 'You've always been the lords of the manor, and you won't accept this is the end of the twentieth century, and things have changed. Well, it's about time you realised no one's going to scrape and bow to you any more just because you're the Earl of Sherringborne. And especially not me!'

A dangerous glitter showed briefly in James's eyes and he took a step forward. Then he stopped and stood still, everything tightly under control again, but there was a perceptible edge to his voice when he next spoke.

'I don't think that I've asked you to do anything unreasonable. I've arranged for you to be driven from the airport to Sherringborne Manor—for your own convenience—and offered to take you to your flat *en route* so that you can pick up some extra luggage.'

Philippa had to admit that, put like that, it didn't sound unreasonable at all. Or was he just being clever with words? She suspected that this man was very clever indeed, and in ways that she didn't even know about yet.

All the same, she began to feel slightly ashamed of her outburst. What on earth would Jonathan think if he ever found out that she was being so obstructive? Especially since she was only behaving like this because of James Haverford's infuriating attitude! And it *would* be a lot easier if she had a car to take her and her luggage to the Manor.

'All right,' she said at last through gritted teeth, forcing out the words because she hated losing an argument to this man, 'I'll accept your offer, Lord Sherringborne.'

'If we're going to be related by marriage, perhaps we should practise using each other's Christian name,' he suggested coolly. 'Jonathan may think it rather strange if we're still addressing each other as Lord Sherringborne and Miss Martin by the time he returns.'

'I don't see why our relationship shouldn't stay completely formal,' she retorted. 'I'm engaged to Jonathan, not his family.' At the same time, though, without even realising that she was doing it, she nervously licked her lips. The thought of addressing this man by his Christian name was surprisingly unsettling.

'The subject of your engagement to my nephew is something that interests me very much,' James said softly. 'I'd like to know exactly how it happened.'

Something about his tone of voice threw Philippa straight back on to the defensive. She didn't know how he had done it, but he had made it sound as if she had used some kind of trickery to ensnare his nephew!

'Jonathan proposed and I accepted,' she said very stiffly. 'It was as simple as that.'

'Relationships are never simple,' James observed, his gaze boring directly into her. 'There are always undercurrents, subtle manipulations—temptations.'

Philippa rose to the challenge immediately. 'And what do you mean by *that*?' she demanded.

James ignored her question. Instead he kept his eyes locked on to her face, his face illuminated only by the huge moon overhead.

'You've a very pretty mouth,' he observed in a dispassionate tone. 'Does it do anything special?'

Too late, she realised what he intended doing. By then, he had already bent his head and let his own mouth briefly explore her lips.

Outraged, Philippa pulled back.

'What do you think you're doing?' she gasped, annoyed—and rather alarmed—by her sudden breathlessness.

'I'd have thought that was fairly obvious. I'm trying to discover how you bewitched Jonathan.' He stepped forward swiftly and his mouth returned for a second kiss, a little more forceful than the first, and Philippa found her mouth opening involuntarily under his, allowing him to explore more deeply, his tongue sending unexpected shivers right through her. Then he abruptly released her again.

'Yes, I can see that Jonathan might find that exciting,' he remarked in the same detached voice. And yet his breathing wasn't quite as steady as it had been a few moments ago.

'You are Jonathan's *uncle*,' she reminded him fiercely. 'How dare you do something like that?'

James smiled, and something about that smile sent a shiver right down the entire length of Philippa's spine.

'I'm not just Jonathan's uncle. I'm also his guardian,' he told her, sending a fresh shock right through her. 'And it's my duty to protect him in every way I can.' His eyes bored into her with sudden intensity. 'I think that we both know the truth about your relationship with Jonathan,' he said, his voice abruptly turning hard. 'But before you start protesting that you really love him, and he's everything you've ever wanted, here's something for you to think about. I have the title. I own the estates and most of the family wealth. Jonathan is certainly my heir, but I have every intention of living for a very long time. He will be an old, old man before he inherits. And in the meantime I may marry and have children. That would cut Jonathan out completely; all he would have then would be his charm and his looks.' James looked at her with all the cynicism in the world gleaming darkly in his eyes. 'I think you're just beginning to realise, pretty little Philippa with the mouth that kisses so nicely, that you've chased after and caught the wrong Haverford.'

Hours later, Philippa was still furious at his accusation that she was only interested in Jonathan because she thought he had money and influence. And she was equally furious at herself, because she couldn't forget that kiss that James had given her. She could still seem to feel the hot imprint of it on her mouth. That was ridiculous, she lectured herself angrily, because no one could feel a kiss hours after it had happened!

She didn't change her mind about going to Sherringborne Manor, though. Now that she had made the decision, she wasn't going to let anyone—and especially not the Earl of Sherringborne!—make her back out. Anyway, she knew that she wanted to meet the rest of Jonathan's family, wanted to see his home, learn more about his background. She realised that she was beginning to be consumed with curiosity about the Haverford family. Jonathan had told her so little—their time together had been just one long round of frivolous fun, and there really hadn't been any opportunity to discuss anything in the least serious.

Her last couple of days in Tunisia passed quickly. She was able to relax and enjoy them because James had returned to England the morning after that scene on the beach. She hadn't even seen him again. She convinced herself that she was pleased he had gone, but it was funny how tame life suddenly seemed when he wasn't around.

Her friend, Julie, returned to the hotel at the weekend, fully recovered from her injury, and they spent the evening exchanging news. Philippa didn't mention either James or Jonathan Haverford, though. They were her own private problem, and one that she had convinced herself she could sort out without help from anyone.

She was due to fly back to England the following morning. Julie went to the airport with her, and Philippa said a reluctant goodbye to her friend, and to Tunisia. She was about to step into the unknown, and she had to admit that she was feeling nervous.

After the plane had landed, she collected her luggage and went through Customs. Then she began to haul her heavy cases towards the taxi rank.

Halfway there, she suddenly stopped as she remembered that James Haverford was going to send a car for her. How was she supposed to recognise it, though? Perhaps it had a crest on its side, she told herself with a wry grin. She supposed the Haverford family must have a crest of some kind. It was probably something very impressive, with lots of rampant lions or fierce-eyed eagles!

While she was still standing there, an older man in an immaculate uniform with matching cap came over to her.

'Miss Martin?' he enquired politely.

'Yes,' she confirmed.

'I am Richardson. Your chauffeur,' he added helpfully as he took her luggage from her.

Philippa's eyebrows shot up. If this was the chauffeur, she couldn't wait to see the car!

She wasn't disappointed. It was a huge Bentley, with gleaming paintwork, and silver chrome that had been polished to such perfection that its brightness almost hurt her eyes. She told the chauffeur the address of her flat in London, then sank back into the leather seat, determined to enjoy every moment of her journey in such unashamed luxury.

Once she reached her flat, she quickly packed some extra clothes, threw in a few personal items that she thought she might need, and then went to tell her neighbour, Mrs Mackie, that she would be away for a while longer. When she went back out to the car, she could see curtains twitching all down the road. Philippa grinned. Her neighbours would all think that she had hooked a millionaire!

As the car purred out of London, she leant forward to speak to the chauffeur.

'Have you worked for the Haverford family long, Mr Richardson?' she asked.

'Just call me Richardson,' he told her. 'And yes, I've worked for them ever since I left school. My father was chauffeur to the present Earl's father, and I took over when he retired. Before that, I was a footman.'

'The Haverfords still have footmen?' Philippa said in disbelief. 'For heaven's sake, this is the twentieth century!'

Richardson smiled. 'Nowadays, it's a rather fancy name for a jack-of-all-trades. I did general repairs around the house and grounds, drove the cars when they needed an extra driver, waited at table at formal dinners—in fact I turned my hand to just about anything. And I still do.'

'How many staff does the Haverford family employ?' Philippa asked, her curiosity completely aroused by now.

'Quite a few. There's the butler, the cook, the housekeeper, several part-time maids and cleaning staff, a couple of general footmen, and the gardeners. That's just the people who work at the house, of course. There are many more employed on the actual estate.'

'Of course,' Philippa echoed faintly. She had pictured Sherringborne Manor as a small country house, with just the family in residence and perhaps a couple of part-time staff. She was beginning to realise that she was going to have to repaint that picture!

'The Haverford family owns a lot of land,' Richardson told her. 'Not as much as they used to—death duties always take a heavy toll, and it's usually land that has to be sold to pay them—but they're still one of the major landowners in the country.'

He said it with a great deal of pride. He obviously had a very high regard for his employers.

Philippa decided that she didn't approve at all of all these people working so hard, so that one man—the Earl of Sherringborne—could live in privileged luxury. She held her tongue, though. She didn't want to upset Richardson by voicing her views out loud. He was obviously very happy with the situation.

The car sped on, past rolling green hills and fields coloured with corn or dotted with sheep. Then Richardson slowed his speed as the car began to pass through small, picturesque villages, with cottages grouped around a church with a solid square tower. The main roads were left behind, and they followed narrow lanes fringed with trees that let through thin shafts of golden sunshine. The sky was clear, and Philippa enjoyed the gentle warmth of the summer sun, which was such a contrast to Tunisia's fierce heat. They were in the heart of Dorset now, little more than an hour's drive from London, but the sleepy, peaceful countryside seemed like another world in contrast to the noisy, crowded city they had just left behind.

Richardson swung the car smoothly to the right, and they passed through an impressive gateway. High, elaborate wrought-iron gates were attached to tall carved pillars. The gates stood open, so they were obviously expected.

Beyond the gates, a gravel drive swept through rolling stretches of lawn shaded by great spreading chestnut trees, gnarled oaks and glorious copper beeches, their deep purple leaves a rich mass of colour as they shone darkly in the sunshine.

Then the house itself came into view and Philippa immediately caught her breath. It was very old, very beautiful—and quite magnificent!

The stone walls were a soft creamy grey, highlighted with gold around the long windows with their fine tracery. Mock battlements fringed the upper floor, and stone griffins glared down fiercely from the corners of the roof. Tall, dark yew hedges hid the private gardens that spread out around the rear of the house, but open archways cut into them gave tantalising glimpses of flowers tumbling over narrow paths, foliage that was gold, silver and every shade of green, and the distant glint of water.

Sherringborne Manor was staggeringly impressive, and the sheer size of it was *very* intimidating. Philippa found that she was biting her lower lip nervously as she got out of the car.

'Go straight in,' Richardson said, with a friendly smile. 'You're expected. I'll bring your luggage in later.'

She took a deep breath, then walked steadily towards the great porch that led into the house. The carved wooden door with a massive ornamental knocker stood ajar, and she hesitantly went inside.

Philippa found herself standing in what had to be the Great Hall. The timbered roof soared high above her, and beams of patterned light filtered through the heraldic stained-glass windows. Dark oak, heavily carved furniture stood on the cream stone floor, the two colours contrasting perfectly. Linenfold panelling covered the bottom half of the walls, a huge tapestry hung over the biggest fireplace Philippa had ever seen, and a gothic chandelier hung over head, suspended from a chain bolted to the great central beam in the roof.

She was still gazing at it all in some awe when a familiar voice made her jump.

'So, you've come.'

Philippa spun round to face the Earl of Sherringborne, and found that just the sight of him made her pulses race in the most alarming way. It was that kiss, she told herself shakily. He shouldn't have done it; he had no right to touch me! Or say the things he did.

She lifted her head defiantly. 'Of course. I said that I would, and I don't break my word.'

A cynical smile crossed James's face. 'I never thought that you would. I was sure that you wouldn't want to miss the opportunity to check out Jonathan's background and inspect the family assets. Well?' he challenged her, his eyes gleaming brilliant blue. 'Does the house come up to expectations? Is it big enough, grand enough for you?'

'The kind of home that Jonathan lives in isn't in the least important to me,' she said hotly. 'I wouldn't care if he lived in a one-room flat in the middle of the suburbs!' Then she was immediately furious with herself for letting him get to her like this, the moment she had walked in the door. She should have simply ignored his cutting remarks.

James walked slowly forward. He was wearing jeans and a leather jacket, and the modern clothes should have looked completely out of place in this beautiful and ancient house, yet they didn't. Philippa had the feeling that the Earl of Sherringborne would never look out of place anywhere.

'Would you like to take a look at the rest of the house?' he invited, his gaze still glowing brightly and never leaving her face. 'See the silver, the famous paintings, the priceless antiques?'

'I'm not interested in your family wealth,' Philippa said through gritted teeth.

'Everyone's interested in money,' he said caustically. 'Especially when there's so much of it.' Then his tone changed, became crisper, more detached. 'But if you want to go on pretending that none of this means anything to you, I'll take you up to your room.'

'Shouldn't the butler do that?' Philippa retorted as she followed him towards the wide doorway at the far end of the hall, under the minstrel's gallery.

'The butler has more important things to do,' James replied coolly.

Philippa glared at his back as she followed him out of the hall. She had only been here a few minutes and he had already managed to ruffle her temper completely!

He led her up a wide spiral staircase that took them up to the first floor. The treads under her feet were solid oak, worn in the centre with the constant passage of feet over the centuries, and portraits of Haverford ancestors looked down at her with what seemed to her to be extreme disapproval from the walls.

Upstairs, there was more dark panelling, and yet it certainly wasn't a gloomy house. Golden sunlight streamed in through the lattice windows, the old carpets had faded over the years to soft colours, the wood itself gleamed richly, and bowls of freshly cut flowers brightened shadowed corners.

James stopped in front of one of the doors and opened it. 'This will be your room during your stay here.'

Philippa walked inside, and then her eyes opened very wide. The bed was a four-poster, with elaborately carved columns at each corner that supported a fringed and tasselled canopy. There was an oak chest at the foot of the bed, a couple of chairs with barley-sugar-twist arms and legs, a footstool, and a table with a couple of heavy candlesticks standing on it.

'You may need the candles,' James told her. 'The electricity sometimes cuts out without any warning.'

'Poor maintenance?' she said, her eyebrows delicately rising.

'Maybe it's just one of the family ghosts, objecting to the way that certain parts of the house have been modernised,' he replied, his eyes glinting. 'Are you afraid of ghosts, Miss Martin? I do hope that you don't have a nervous disposition.'

'I'm not afraid of *anything*,' she said at once. And that had been more or less the truth—until she had met James Haverford! 'And I thought that we agreed to use Christian names?' she reminded him boldly.

'So we did,' he agreed. 'Very well, then—Philippa.'

The instant he said her name, every nerve in her body felt as if it had just done a complete somersault! Philippa was absolutely pole-axed by her reaction—and terrified that he would notice it.

She began to talk nervously, trying to cover up her total confusion. 'And I suppose I'd better practise calling you James.' Her tongue slid so easily over his own name, she only just stopped herself licking her lips in the secret pleasure of saying it. 'After all,' she jabbered on, more and more unnerved by what was happening to her, 'if I marry Jonathan, you'll be my—what? Uncle-in-law?'

James's gaze instantly sharpened. '*If* you marry Jonathan?' he repeated, ignoring everything else she had said. 'Is it in some doubt? I thought you had every intention of marching him to the altar as soon as he returns from the Himalayas. Is there some problem?'

She had made a serious mistake and forgotten how very clever he was. Only one person in a hundred would have picked up her small slip of the tongue.

'No problem at all,' she denied at once. She still had absolutely no intention of admitting to James that she had growing doubts about her engagement. That was something very private that she had to resolve for herself before Jonathan returned. And she hoped that being here, in his home, would help her to do that.

James continued to stare directly at her, though, as if trying to see right inside her head. Philippa somehow found the nerve to stand her ground and stare right back at him. She was determined not to flinch, or let him see how completely disconcerting she found it when he focused his attention on her with such intensity.

'There's something not quite right here,' he said at last. 'And I intend to find out what it is,' he warned softly, sending a ripple of apprehension right through her. 'But, in the meantime, you're a guest in this house, and you have to be treated as such. Dinner is at six o'clock. Please try and be prompt as my mother is joining us for the meal. She wants to meet you.'

'Your—your mother?' Philippa repeated with a fresh wave of nervousness.

James smiled at her, the kind of smile that made her knees suddenly begin to shake.

'We have some questions that we'd like to ask you, Philippa,' he said gently. 'We're very interested in you.'

'What do you mean—interested?' she asked with a small gulp.

He seemed to be standing much closer than before, and she couldn't understand it because she was *sure* that he hadn't moved. He bent his head a little; she could see every detail of his mouth now, hard and well-shaped. She could almost taste his lips——

Philippa swallowed convulsively and, suddenly panic-stricken, told herself to stop. What on earth was she doing even letting herself *think* about his mouth? And what it could do!

She told herself to back off, do it now, before she got involved in something disastrous—like another kiss. But she was frozen to the spot, absolutely couldn't move.

And James's mouth was only inches away now, and she couldn't stop staring at it as it moved closer—and closer.

CHAPTER THREE

AT THE very last moment, James stopped and froze, as if he had only just realised what he intended doing. His self-control slammed back into place, but not before the hot glow of frustration had begun to burn in his eyes.

'Oh, no,' he said forcefully, 'you don't play those kind of games with me!'

'What games?' asked Philippa in confusion.

'Don't act the innocent,' he ordered roughly. 'Remember, I'm not Jonathan. I've more than enough experience to deal with a little temptress like you.'

Temptress? she thought in growing bewilderment.

'You've plenty of time to unpack,' he told her in a low growl. 'We'll meet at dinner again this evening.'

Then he swiftly left the room, leaving Philippa's head whirling.

What was happening? she asked herself in some alarm. Every time they met, the sparks began to fly!

Then a light rap on the door sent her fractured nerves spinning turbulently all over again. She tried to calm herself but it was impossible, because she knew that it might be James back again.

When she finally tottered over on shaky legs and opened the door, though, it was only Richardson with her bags.

'Settling in?' he asked with a friendly smile as he set down her luggage.

Her heart finally settled down to an almost normal rhythm. 'Not really,' she admitted. 'Everything's—well, bigger, much grander than I expected.' And far more disturbing than this magnificent house, of course, was Lord Sherringborne himself. She didn't intend to tell Richardson that, though. She didn't even like admitting it to herself!

'Don't let the grandeur of the house bother you,' Richardson advised. Then, as if guessing what else was disturbing her, he added, 'And I know that the Haverfords can be rather intimidating when you first meet them—particularly Lord Sherringborne—but underneath they're really very nice people.'

'Nice?' Philippa repeated disbelievingly. 'James Haverford is *nice*?'

'Perhaps that wasn't quite the right word,' Richardson said with a dry smile. 'His Lordship's got a fierce temper and a very strong will, but he's usually a fair man. And very clever. He needs to be, of course. Running an estate this size and keeping it financially solvent isn't at all easy these days.'

'I've got to meet his mother this evening,' Philippa said with a fresh rush of trepidation. 'She's coming to dinner. What should I wear? And what do I call her?'

'Just call her Lady Haverford. Officially, she's the Dowager Countess of Sherringborne, but no one uses that rather old-fashioned title. And just wear something simple,' Richardson told her. 'It's only a family meal, so you don't need to dress up.'

'I'll probably use the wrong knives and forks,' she predicted gloomily.

'Always work from the outside inwards. And if you do get it wrong, don't worry about it. Nearly everyone does it sometimes. No one will laugh at you.'

Except James Haverford, Philippa thought ruefully. She was quite sure that he would give a superior little smile!

She was sorry to see Richardson go: he seemed to be the only friendly face around here. She slowly started to unpack, and at the same time tried to decide what to wear for dinner tonight.

In the end, she settled for a plain straight skirt which looked very demure until she moved. Then the long slit up the side revealed a length of tanned, slim leg. She teamed it with a soft silk shirt which she had bought at a drastically reduced price in a sale. She drew her glossy brown hair back from her face and secured it with a velvet band, dusted her eyes with shadow, subtly highlighted her cheekbones, and lightly coloured the generous line of her mouth. Then she critically studied her reflection.

Satisfied that she looked suitably dressed to have dinner with an earl and a dowager countess, she took a deep breath and left the bedroom.

The evening sun was filling the house with a golden light. Philippa was already falling head over heels in love with Sherringborne Manor. The house had bewitched her from the moment she had first set eyes on it; she could very happily live here for the rest of her days—if it weren't filled with Haverfords!

She found her way to the Great Hall, but wasn't sure where the dining-room was. A glance at her watch warned her that it was nearly six o'clock, and she bit her lower lip a little anxiously. She didn't want to be late for her first meeting with Jonathan's grandmother.

The door at the far end of the Great Hall swung open, and Philippa gave a small sigh of relief. It was probably one of the household staff. She would ask for directions to the dining-room.

It was James who walked in, though. The jeans and leather jacket had been replaced by a dark evening suit, and he looked very formal and unapproachable.

As he came towards her, his blue eyes travelled the length of her body, critically assessing every inch.

Once Philippa had got over the first shock of seeing him—were her nerves *always* going to turn over like that at the sight of him? she wondered apprehensively—she became annoyed at his open inspection of her appearance.

'Well?' she said, forcing herself to return his stare without flinching. 'Am I suitably dressed to meet your mother?'

'Of course,' he said. 'But I thought that you would be. You'll obviously want to make a good impression on her, since she's also Jonathan's grandmother.'

Philippa could clearly hear the cynical note back in his voice again, and she felt the heat beginning to build up in her own face. Did he think that everything she did had an ulterior motive?

The answer to that was obviously yes! She bit back her angry reply, though, and tried to force herself to be cool, keep calm. There was still her first meeting with Lady Haverford to get through, and she was absolutely determined that it was going to go well. If she wanted to marry Jonathan, then she had to get on well with the rest of his family.

'If'—that word seemed to be creeping in an awful lot lately. She really had to try and be more positive about her engagement, she told herself.

She realised that James's eyes were still locked on to her, which made a fresh wave of heat wash over her. He hadn't moved another inch towards her and outwardly he looked very relaxed, but she still felt threatened by him. Not physically threatened; it was something a lot more subtle than that. He undermined her peace of mind; he could ruffle all her nerve-ends simply by *looking* at her. And, to make it worse, she was quite sure that he knew exactly what effect he had on her.

'Shouldn't we be going to the dining-room?' she said in a voice that, to her annoyance, came out as a nervous croak.

A gleam of satisfaction briefly showed in his eyes, as if he enjoyed being able to reduce her to this state. Then it disappeared again.

'It's this way,' he told her, his own voice crisp and completely under control. He led her out of the Great Hall, along a narrow passage, and then through a door that led into a large, airy room. Windows opened on to the gardens at the back of the house, and the scent of flowers and the sound of birdsong floated softly into the room. The walls of the room were covered with silk, the carpet under her feet was a complex pattern of soft colours, and the furniture was dark and elegant.

Philippa's gaze was fixed on the dining-table, though. It stretched almost the entire length of the room! It would have seated a couple of dozen people comfortably, but tonight just three chairs were set around it, one at each end and the third in the middle.

This obviously wasn't going to be a cosy meal, she told herself with fast sinking spirits.

Then she held her breath nervously because the door at the other end of the room had just opened. A second later, a tall, handsome, older woman came in, walking slowly and leaning heavily on a stick. Philippa's heart sank even lower than her spirits as she saw the silver hair immaculately set around pale but very autocratic features, and the distinctive, brilliant blue Haverford eyes. It certainly wasn't a friendly or welcoming face! Lady Haverford's dress was dark, severe, and so beautifully cut that it had clearly cost a fortune. Just a single strand of perfect pearls lightened its severity, and Philippa was very glad that she hadn't chosen to wear anything bright and glitzy. She was absolutely certain that Lady Haverford would have radiated instant disapproval.

Lady Haverford walked over a little haltingly, stopped in front of Philippa, and then treated her to the same critical head-to-toe inspection that she had endured from James just minutes ago. Despite her physical frailty, her mind was obviously completely clear and sharp. Philippa gritted her teeth and told herself that she *didn't* mind this open scrutiny; Jonathan's grandmother was bound to be curious about her.

'So, you're Philippa Martin,' Lady Haverford said at last. 'Jonathan's fiancée. His announcement of his engagement came as rather a surprise to all of us.' And not an entirely pleasant surprise, her tone intimated. 'How did you meet my grandson?'

Philippa hadn't expected such a direct question only moments after meeting Lady Haverford, and she blurted out the answer without thinking.

'I popped out of a cake and Jonathan was standing there, right in front of me.'

Lady Haverford's perfectly shaped eyebrows slowly rose. 'You—popped out of a cake?'

Philippa could feel a hot flush of colour sweeping right across her face, and she was quite certain that, very soon, she was going to wish that she had never set foot in this house, never met anyone who went by the name of Haverford.

'It—it was a party,' she stammered, getting more and more flustered. 'A birthday party. Jonathan was one of the guests. I'd been hired to pop out of this giant cake and sing "Happy Birthday". It isn't the kind of thing I usually do, but I was in between jobs and short of money, so...'

Her voice trailed away. What was the point of trying to make these wealthy people understand what it was like to have the rent due, bills to be paid, and no money coming in? OK, so it wasn't the best job in the world, to jump out of a cake in a silly, frilly costume and sing 'Happy Birthday' to a complete stranger, but it was better than being evicted because the rent was overdue!

Lady Haverford was now looking at her as if she had come to Sherringborne Manor from another planet.

'How interesting,' she said at last in a frosty voice.

'I think that we would both like to hear more about your colourful career,' James said, his vivid blue eyes boring into her. 'You will, after all, soon be a Haverford, and I don't think that any member of our family has ever been a belly-dancer. Or jumped out of a giant cake. Are there any more surprises that we don't yet know about?'

His tone clearly warned that there had better not be. Philippa suddenly felt totally alone and horribly vulnerable. How on earth was she going to get through the rest of this evening with this arrogant man and his frail but intimidatingly haughty mother?

They sat down to dinner soon after that. Philippa was glad of the chance to sink into a chair, because she didn't want them to see that her legs had begun to shake.

James sat at the head of the table, and Lady Haverford at the other end. Philippa was seated in the middle, caught between those two intensely blue Haverford gazes. As soon as the wine had been poured, she hurriedly gulped down a couple of mouthfuls. She definitely needed something to steady her nerves!

The first course was a simple starter of soup. The meal was served by a middle-aged woman in a neat black dress and crisp white apron. When she had left the room again, Lady Haverford raised her head and addressed Philippa.

'Have you set a date for the wedding?' She was obviously used to asking very direct questions—and seemed to expect equally straightforward answers.

'Er—no, not really——' Philippa began evasively, desperately hoping that she wasn't going to have to spend the evening fielding questions about a wedding that might never even take place.

'Jonathan gave us very little information about you, before he went away,' James cut in. 'Perhaps you'd like to fill in some details?'

Philippa knew that a rebellious spark had suddenly begun to flicker in her brown eyes. She was, after all, meant to be a guest here. Instead of being welcoming or friendly, though, the Haverfords obviously had every intention of spending the evening interrogating her at some length!

'Perhaps we could finish our meal before I embark on my life history,' she said in a brittle tone.

'Why?' enquired James coolly. 'I assume that you're capable of eating *and* talking?'

'I'm capable of a great many things,' she retorted, rising to the challenge. 'And if you're really interested in the story of my life, here's a potted version. I had a restricted childhood because I was an only child and my parents always wanted to keep me wrapped in cotton wool. I didn't enjoy my teens because it was one long battle to lead any kind of normal life, but I did manage it at least some of the time. My parents died when I was eighteen and I still miss them like mad because I loved them, even though they nearly drove me mad at times. I've led a very independent life since then, and I've worked hard at my career as a dancer. When there isn't any work—which happens quite often—I'll take any job that comes along so that I can carry on paying the rent. Including jumping out of cakes!' She met James's gaze boldly as she said that, and there was a faint note of defiance in her voice. Then she realised that her gaze was sliding down involuntarily to the hard, beautiful line of his mouth. Why couldn't she stop staring at it? To her intense dismay, she found herself remembering that kiss on the beach in Tunisia, and gave herself a quick mental shake. This was no time to be thinking of such things!

James's expression had changed perceptibly during her recital. 'You're completely on your own?' he said with a small frown.

'Not quite. I've a couple of elderly aunts in Scotland, although I hardly ever see them. And I think I've a distant cousin in America, but we've completely lost touch. But don't start feeling sorry for me,' she warned. 'I *like* being independent; I manage perfectly well on my own. I've some good friends, a career that I thoroughly enjoy most of the time and a home of my own. My life is fine, at the moment.'

She was exaggerating quite a lot, of course. 'Home' was a tiny, one-bedroomed flat, and her career didn't seem to be going anywhere at the moment—except down! Pride was forcing her to put on a good front, though; she didn't want this man to see the vulnerable side of her, the side that was often lonely, uncertain, and sometimes even frightened. Vulnerability was a weakness that she was afraid he would quite ruthlessly exploit.

But James wasn't offering any sympathy. Instead he sat back and regarded her levelly. The light overhead glinted off his gleaming dark hair, and his elegant hands with the long, sure fingers played casually with the silver cutlery. 'Yes, I'm sure that you're very pleased with your life,' he remarked. 'Especially since you met Jonathan.'

If it had been anyone else who had said that, she would have thought he was simply congratulating her on meeting someone who made her happy. But Philippa found she was tuned in to the hidden undercurrents in his voice, and she immediately reacted.

'What do you mean by that?' she demanded.

'I'm quite sure that you've told the truth about being a very capable and independent girl. You know what you want, and you go straight after it. And my guess is that you usually get it. There are few things more satisfying than achieving your aims. Don't you agree?' he challenged her softly, his gaze locking on to hers with sudden brilliance.

Philippa wished that he wouldn't suddenly lower his voice like that, his tone turning to pure velvet and hitting a note that made the fine hairs on her skin stand right up on end! She certainly knew what he was insinuating, though. 'You're talking about my relationship with Jonathan, aren't you?' she said hotly. 'You're accusing me of deliberately chasing after him. You think that I want him because of the background he comes from, all the money, stately homes and titles!'

Lady Haverford finally stepped in. 'This hardly seems a suitable conversation for the dinner-table.'

Philippa swung round and looked at her with a swift blaze of defiance, furiously blinking back the angry tears from her eyes.

'I don't think that's my fault! I thought this was going to be a pleasant family dinner, where we could all get to know each other a little better. In fact, I hoped you were going to turn out to be an ordinary family, despite your grand house and imposing titles. I was very wrong, though, wasn't I? Not one person has said a pleasant word to me since I set foot in Sherringborne Manor. Except for Richardson, and he's just a servant, isn't he? I suppose he's allowed to be nice to me!' Her gaze shot back to James's swiftly darkening face as the words kept pouring out of her. 'Perhaps you think that's where I belong, in the servants' quarters? You certainly don't want your precious Jonathan to *marry* someone like me, do you? Someone whose father was just a clerk. Someone who belly-dances in hotels when she's short of money. Well, sorry, but that's who I am! And I'm proud of it. I like the person I am, and I don't care if you think I'm unsuitable to join your precious family. Your opinion simply doesn't matter to me!'

She had scrambled to her feet and, because she was absolutely determined not to give them the satisfaction of seeing her cry, she made a dash for the door as soon as she had flung those last few words at them. Somehow she managed to hold back the furious flood of tears until she was out of the room.

She kept on going, finding the stairs by pure luck because she could hardly see by now—her eyes were too blurred. She stumbled up them, managed to make it back to her bedroom, and slammed the door shut behind her.

'Stop crying, *stop* it,' she ordered herself fiercely, rubbing her eyes hard. 'The Haverfords aren't worth a single tear!'

She rushed into the adjoining bathroom, where cold water splashed over her face helped to wash away the humiliating tears. Philippa shook her head as she gradually got herself back under control again. She couldn't believe how awful that dinner had been—and they hadn't even got past the first course!

She went back into the bedroom and wondered what she should do now. Run away? But she hated admitting defeat. All the same, it was going to be very difficult staying here if she couldn't win over one single member of Jonathan's family. And it didn't seem as if she was going to have much luck with his grandmother, Lady Haverford. She might look physically frail, but that didn't stop her from being almost as formidable as her son!

An authoritative rap on the door broke into her thoughts and made her jump. Before she had a chance to ask who it was, the door swung open and James walked in.

He was still wearing the immaculately cut suit and crisp white shirt he'd worn for dinner, but even if he had been wearing the most casual of clothes he would still have looked every inch an earl—someone who could trace his ancestors back for generations. It was something about his supremely confident bearing, his absolute faith in his ability to handle every situation, the way he walked into a room as if he had a perfect right to be there. Philippa found herself gulping hard as her gaze was drawn to him. It wasn't *fair*, she thought a little resentfully. This whole thing would have been so much easier to cope with if he had been short, old and ugly! Every time she was confronted by him unexpectedly, her entire nervous system just threatened to collapse!

She had to make a huge effort to give him an unfriendly glare.

'I didn't invite you in here!'

'This is my house. I don't need an invitation. But I don't intend to stay. I merely came up to ask you if you wanted to return to the dining-room to finish your dinner.'

'Finish my dinner?' she repeated incredulously. Was he crazy? How could she even *think* of eating, after that awful scene in the dining-room?

'I didn't expect you to be so frightened by us that you'd run out during the first course,' James commented.

'I'm not frightened of you at all,' Philippa denied at once, aware that she was lying through her teeth. 'I was just spitting mad. And I certainly didn't intend to stay there and be insulted!'

'I don't remember anyone insulting you. There was some plain speaking—on all sides—but no one was actually rude to you.'

'That isn't how I remember it!' she retorted. 'And your mother's attitude made it perfectly plain how she felt about me.'

'She simply wanted to know more about you. I don't see anything wrong in that. And there was certainly no need to over-react in the way that you did.'

'Over-react?' Philippa echoed with fresh indignation. 'I think I was very restrained!'

'Then it would be interesting to see you when you're being uninhibited,' James said, his eyes briefly gleaming. 'And you might like to know that my mother was far more impressed with you than she expected. She was quite certain that you would be very pretty, very empty-headed and very boring.'

'Why?'

'Because most of Jonathan's previous girlfriends have fallen into that category. He's still very young, and he usually goes for looks, not brains.'

She had the feeling that, in a roundabout way, he had just paid her a compliment, and she had to work hard to suppress a traitorous wave of pleasure.

'I think Jonathan is very mature for his age,' she said loyally.

James's dark eyebrows gently rose. 'Then you obviously didn't get to know my nephew very well before he dashed off to the Himalayas.' Before she could contradict that remark, he went on, 'I don't intend to keep the staff waiting around all evening. If you want to finish your meal, come back to the dining-room right now.'

'I'm not setting foot in that room again,' she said at once, ignoring the faint rumbling in her stomach as it tried to remind her that she hadn't eaten a proper meal all day.

'You'll be very hungry if you don't eat.'

'That's my problem. Anyway, I can always go down to the kitchen and make myself a couple of sandwiches. I suppose that is allowed?' she enquired with a touch of sarcasm.

'No, it isn't,' James replied coolly. 'Mrs Williams is a first-class cook, but very temperamental. Every time someone sets foot inside her kitchen without permission, she threatens to hand in her notice.'

'And you allow her to get away with that?' she asked in amazement. She hadn't thought that anyone on this earth could ever get the better of James Haverford!

'Good cooks are very hard to find, and even harder to keep,' he said drily. 'I've already had to placate her this evening because you ruined dinner by rushing out before the first course was even over.'

'Well, I'm sorry, I wouldn't have done it if I'd known it would upset the cook!' she retorted. At the same time, though, she could feel her attitude softening. She had to admit that she *hadn't* behaved very well. Neither had they, of course, she reminded herself swiftly, but that didn't really excuse her outburst. 'If I do come down, I suppose I'll have to apologise to your mother?' she added, with a definite lack of enthusiasm.

'My mother's gone home. She decided that she'd had enough excitement for one evening.'

Philippa gave a silent sigh of relief. That was one less hurdle to face.

'Does she live near by?' she asked. Not too near, she hoped. She didn't want her popping back unexpectedly! She didn't think that she could cope with James *and* his mother again this evening.

'She has her own cottage in the grounds, a couple of miles away from the main house.'

'A cottage?' she echoed in surprise. She couldn't picture the elegant, autocratic Dowager Countess of Sherringborne living in a cosy little house with roses round the door.

'It was built a couple of hundred years ago by one of the earlier Earls of Sherringborne. He wanted a quiet retreat, when the woman he married turned out to be a nagging shrew! It's on a much smaller scale than this house, of course—just half a dozen bedrooms, a drawing-room, reception-room, dining-room, kitchen and large conservatory.'

Philippa's eyebrows shot up. 'And that's what you call a cottage?'

'It's a very large cottage,' James conceded.

'Everything around here is very large,' she said with some feeling. 'Including that table in the dining-room. I felt as if I was sitting half a mile away from everyone!'

'Considering the way you obviously feel about us, I would have thought you preferred it that way,' James said pointedly. Then he glanced at his watch. 'Dinner should be ready by now. Let's go and eat before the food's ruined all over again and I have another domestic crisis on my hands.'

With some reluctance, Philippa followed him downstairs, back to the dining-room. When she went inside, she found that the seating arrangement had been changed. Instead of sitting at the head of the table, James was now seated opposite her.

Philippa wasn't at all sure that she liked that. Minutes ago, she had been very hungry. Now, with those vivid blue Haverford eyes facing her directly from just a couple of feet away, she felt her appetite quickly slipping away.

A fresh bowl of soup was placed in front of her. She broke her roll, but then dropped a large piece of it straight into her soup, sending small spots splattering out in all directions over the immaculate white tablecloth. She rubbed at them a little frantically with her napkin, but that only smudged them and made them look far worse.

'Leave it,' James ordered. 'The cloth can easily be washed.' Then his dark brows drew together thoughtfully. 'Why do I make you so nervous?'

'You don't,' Philippa lied at once, absolutely determined *never* to admit that he could make her shake from head to foot just by looking at her. 'I'm—I'm tired, that's all. It's been a long and difficult day.'

'If you go ahead with your proposed marriage to Jonathan, you'll probably have a difficult life,' he warned. 'Jonathan's a charming boy, but not very reliable. And he certainly isn't ready to settle down yet.'

'I don't think you should talk about your nephew like that,' she said disapprovingly.

'Why not? I've known Jonathan all his life; I know exactly what he's like. I also know that he doesn't need a wife. He's only twenty years old, and still far too immature to marry.'

'I think that Jonathan should be the one to decide that,' she said stiffly. 'Anyway, plenty of twenty-year-olds get married.'

'And divorced,' James pointed out, his face darkening. His eyes locked on to hers with that intensity that she always found so very disturbing. 'You realise that, as Jonathan's guardian, I could place a great many obstacles in your path?'

'Yes, you could. But he'll be twenty-one in just a few months. You won't have any power over him then,' she retorted.

James's mouth—that beautiful, sensual mouth—hardened perceptibly. 'You're too old for him, Philippa,' he warned. 'Don't use your experience to force Jonathan into a marriage that will almost certainly be a disaster.'

What experience? she thought ruefully. When it came to relationships, she was just a novice. She was never going to admit that to James, though! 'Jonathan wants me,' she told him firmly. Her words seemed to fuel his growing anger, though, and he leant over the table towards her in a threatening posture.

'Jonathan's never really known what he wants,' he said harshly. 'There have been a dozen girls like you. If you break the engagement, he'll find a new one in a week.'

His intimidating attitude, his assumption that he knew what was best for both her and Jonathan, immediately made Philippa very angry. She quite forgot her own growing doubts about this marriage.

'I didn't force him into this engagement!' she reminded him hotly. 'In fact *he* was the one who insisted on it.'

'And what did you do to persuade him?' James challenged her.

From the cynical line of his mouth, Philippa knew perfectly well how he thought she had persuaded him. In bed!

She was about to blurt out that no such thing had happened; that she and Jonathan had never been any further than long but friendly kisses. Then she stopped herself. No, she would *not* tell him that. It was none of his damned business! Let him think what he liked; she wasn't going to discuss her personal life with him.

She pushed her soup aside, almost untouched. 'I've eaten enough, thank you,' she said, forcing her voice to stay rigidly polite.

'Finish your meal,' he growled at her.

Philippa knew that her brown eyes had begun to flash fiercely. 'Don't tell me what to do—not about *anything*.'

James's own gaze intensified again, and a warning glitter appeared in the deep blue depths. 'I'm the head of this family. If you intend to join it, then you'll accept that fact without question. And here's something else for you to think about. Until Jonathan reaches maturity, I've the power of veto over the major decisions in his life. And I'll decide whether I'll allow this marriage to go ahead.'

'Whether you'll allow it?' she repeated incredulously. 'What gives you the right to interfere in someone's life like that?'

'As his guardian, I've the moral right and the legal right,' James reminded her tautly. 'I'm responsible for both Jonathan and his sister, Stephanie.'

A wave of shock ran right through Philippa, making her sit back and blink hard. Sister? Jonathan had a *sister*? He had never told her that!

James's eyes narrowed with sudden suspicion as he studied her face. 'You didn't know about Stephanie?'

'Jonathan—he—well, he never mentioned her. I always assumed he was an—an only child,' she said a little incoherently, quite stunned by this piece of news. 'I suppose it was because—well, we didn't talk much about our families.'

Their few weeks together had been just a non-stop round of fun and parties, frivolous conversation and light-hearted banter. Nothing serious had been allowed to spoil their carefree relationship. Philippa, who had found that being independent meant that life often had to be taken very seriously indeed, had revelled in the sheer pleasure of being totally irresponsible for a short time. Too late, she was beginning to realise that their friendship hadn't been just carefree, but also very shallow.

The look on James's face now made her very glad that there was the solid width of the table between them. She was used to Jonathan's slim, lean build, and James's powerful, formidable build, allied with that strength that was mental as well as physical, was something that she found hard to handle. It was such a lethal combination!

He leant forward again, the dark planes of his face set into fierce, inflexible lines.

'Tell me more about your relationship with Jonathan,' he invited, his tone so soft, and yet it still sent small icy shivers right down her spine. 'I want to know exactly what you did to him to make him forget everything—even his own sister!'

CHAPTER FOUR

'I DIDN'T do *anything*,' Philippa said defensively.

From the hard set of James's mouth, it was clear that he didn't believe her.

'Perhaps he doesn't feel very close to his sister,' she rushed on. 'I know that Jonathan hasn't lived at home for a couple of years; he told me that he moved into his own flat in London when he was eighteen. That must have distanced him from his family.'

A fresh darkness spread over James's face. 'The flat you're referring to is mine. I allow Jonathan to stay there when he's in town. The rest of the time he still lives here, at Sherringborne.'

'Oh,' she said, biting her lower lip. It seemed that Jonathan hadn't been entirely truthful with her. She guessed that he had been trying to sound more independent, more adult, than he actually was.

'You and Jonathan seem to have a very strange relationship,' James said, his voice edged with deep suspicion. 'You don't know about his sister, and you don't even know where he lives.'

'There's nothing strange about it,' she denied, aware that she had put herself in a very vulnerable position. 'We just didn't discuss certain things. Certain *important* things,' she conceded. 'I suppose we were rather selfishly wrapped up in each other.'

For some reason, James didn't seem to like that last remark. His body tensed, and a new, warning glow lit his eyes.

'I'd certainly like to know more about his sister, though,' Philippa hurried on, unnerved by this new show of hostility. 'How—how old is she?'

She didn't think he was going to answer her. 'Stephanie is thirteen,' he growled at last.

'Where is she?' she went on edgily. 'Why haven't I seen her?'

'She's been taking a short holiday with some friends. She'll be home either tomorrow or the day after.'

'I'll look forward to meeting her,' Philippa said. And that was the truth, because she hoped that Stephanie would be just like her brother—friendly and easygoing. It would be so nice to meet a friendly Haverford!

'Stay away from her,' James ordered at once.

'*What*?' she said, not quite believing that he had actually said that.

'Stephanie's at a very impressionable age. I don't want her mixing with anyone who'll influence her in the wrong way.'

'And that means me?' she said, jumping to her feet in outrage.

'Of course.'

'What do you think I am?' she demanded incredulously.

'Don't push me, or I might answer that question,' James warned grimly.

'No, let's get this right out into the open! You've already labelled me a fortune-hunting siren who's managed to trick Jonathan into proposing marriage. And now you're telling me to stay away from your precious niece because I'll have a subversive influence on her? If you weren't serious, the whole thing would be ridiculous and laughable! But you *are* serious, aren't you?' she said, her eyes blazing furiously.

James also got to his feet, towering over her, intimidating her with his sheer size.

'I certainly am,' he said tautly. 'And you'd do well to remember that I don't issue empty threats.' His own gaze bored into her with nerve-jarring force. 'You must have realised by now that all the advantages are on my side, Philippa. You can't fight me. You can't hurt me. You can't touch me in any way. On the other hand, there are a great many things that *I* can do. I can make sure that you are never accepted by any member of this family. I can exert a great deal of influence over Jonathan, and I'll certainly do it if I think it's in his best interests. And I can protect Stephanie and my mother from you. Don't ever think that you can win, if it comes to an outright fight between us. I haven't even begun to show you yet what I'm capable of.'

The air between them seemed to crackle with a dark, electric tension, and every single one of Philippa's nerves felt painfully raw and on edge. She felt physically ill—her skin was very hot and painfully sensitive, as if she was running a high fever. Her stomach was churning, and her breathing was fast and shallow.

But James also seemed to have lost his coolness and self-control. His powerful chest rose and fell in irregular spasms as his own breathing quickened, and she could see a pulse beating very hard in the strong column of his neck. And his mouth was set into such a hard, unyielding line that the colour had drained from his lips.

Philippa stared at their whiteness, not realising that her own mouth—in fact, her entire face—was equally bloodless with tension.

'I didn't come to Sherringborne to fight you,' she managed to get out at last. 'But if it's a fight that you want, then I'm not going to back down. And if you threaten me again I'll promise you one thing. I'll make Jonathan marry me the moment he returns back home. Believe me, I can do it!' she warned, facing up to him with the very last dregs of her courage. 'If Jonathan has to choose between you and me, I'll make very sure that he chooses me. And you won't like *that*, will you?'

Her courage ran out at that point. Issuing a personal challenge to this man was highly dangerous, and the blackness that swept over his face left her under no illusions. She had already pushed him too far!

Philippa turned round and fled from the dining-room for the second time that evening.

She bolted straight up to her room, and locked the door as soon as she was inside.

'Just a precaution,' she breathlessly told herself. 'He wouldn't really come storming up here after me.'

All the same, it was ages before her heart stopped thumping painfully hard. She couldn't quite believe that she had not only had the nerve to stand up to him like that, but had even issued a threat of her own! Of course, it probably hadn't been the wisest thing she had ever done, but it was certainly better than meekly letting him walk all over her.

Philippa found that she couldn't sit still; she kept walking restlessly around the room. Her skin still felt so very hot, and although she tried hard to convince herself that it was because it was a warm night she knew that it really had nothing to do with the temperature.

Every time she heard a strange noise, she jumped edgily. It was only the creaks and groans of the old house, though, and not the sound of footsteps outside her door.

A distant clock chimed eleven o'clock, and then midnight. She had never felt less like sleep in her life. And, despite everything that had happened, she was beginning to feel hungry. Twice tonight she had started dinner, and each time she hadn't managed to get past the first course!

She peered out of the window, and was unnerved all over again by the impenetrable blackness outside. She was a city girl, used to brightly lit city streets, illuminated shop windows and the constant flashes of car headlights.

Her stomach rumbled gently with emptiness, and she rubbed it regretfully. If she were back at her own small flat, she could phone for a pizza. Or pop out for a take-away. She began to think even more longingly of food, and rummaged through her bag, hoping to find a forgotten chocolate bar, or even an apple. She came up with nothing, though.

This is ridiculous, Philippa told herself firmly. You're never going to sleep unless you at least make yourself a hot drink.

With sudden decisiveness, she walked towards the door. She would go down and find the kitchen, and make herself some cocoa. And perhaps a sandwich.

Of course, James had warned her that the cook didn't like anyone even setting foot in her kitchen. But it would be pretty unreasonable of her to object to Philippa's just making a drink. And she would make sure that she cleared everything up very carefully. With luck, no one would even know that she had been there.

She slid her feet into a pair of soft-soled shoes, and quietly opened her bedroom door. Then she gave a small grimace. The house was in complete darkness. She couldn't see a thing! And if she started switching on lights, everyone would come out to see what was going on. There would be the embarrassment of having to explain that she was sneaking down to the kitchen for a midnight snack.

Then Philippa remembered the candles that had been left in her room in case of a power cut. Perfect! she told herself. She found a box of matches in a nearby drawer, lit one of the candles, and then set off through the sleeping house.

Shadows danced and wavered around her as the candle-flame flickered gently. The silence was as eerie as the darkness had been earlier; Philippa wasn't used to such a total lack of noise. Her own small flat was in a busy, crowded part of London, and there was always the sound of traffic, televisions blaring out from nearby flats, or the voices of people walking by. Here, there was nothing except the occasional faint creak of the old house settling even further on to its ancient foundations.

Philippa swallowed hard. 'There aren't any ghosts,' she whispered to herself very softly. 'And even if there were you wouldn't be afraid of them. Just as you're not afraid of the dark. Or of shadows. Or the Earl of Sherringborne!'

All the same, she scuttled down the stairs fairly quickly. Then she clutched her candle even more tightly and began to search for the kitchen. She guessed it was at the back of the house, and after a couple of wrong turns she opened a door at the end of a short corridor and found it.

It was vast! The light from the candle lit barely half of it, leaving the corners in thick black shadow. She could see the great wooden table in the middle, though, and the rows of copper pans and saucepans hanging on the wall, gleaming dully. A huge wood-burning stove dominated the far end of the kitchen, with a massive oven and several hotplates. Philippa was relieved to see there was also a much smaller and more conventional gas stove. She wanted a hot drink, and she didn't want to have to burn half a forest just to heat up a saucepan of milk!

Rather guiltily, she began to search the kitchen for what she needed for her late supper. Although she certainly wasn't doing any harm, it still didn't seem right to be here without permission. Then she forgot about all that as she opened a door and found herself facing the biggest walk-in larder she had even seen. It was stocked with enough food to feed a small army!

The Haverfords either like to eat very well or they do a *lot* of entertaining! she told herself aloud as she looked, wide-eyed, at the rows of shelves absolutely stacked with food.

As well as the larder, there was a massive refrigerator, an even bigger deep freeze, and cupboards and drawers filled with kitchen utensils of every kind.

Everything here was on such a big scale! she thought in amazement. It made her own tiny kitchen look like a child's toy.

She decided that, with all this food, they certainly wouldn't miss a couple of slices of bread and some filling to make a sandwich. She helped herself to a small portion of cold meat from the refrigerator, told herself again that she didn't need to feel guilty, then made her sandwiches and heated up some milk for a mug of cocoa. Finally, she set the candle on the table, and sat down to eat her lonely meal.

When she had finished, she washed up the few things she had used, dried them, and very carefully put them back exactly where she had found them. She examined the table, to make sure that she hadn't left any crumbs behind, and hung the tea-towel to dry over a nearby rail.

Satisfied that she had left the kitchen exactly as she had found it, Philippa turned round to pick up her candle. Then she nearly died of sheer fright as she saw a tall, dark figure standing in the doorway of the kitchen. For a few moments, she thought a long-dead Haverford had come back to haunt her! Then, with a loud gulp, she realised that it was even worse than that. It was James Haverford, very much in the flesh!

'I—er—I——' she stuttered, suddenly incoherent with nerves.

James came further into the kitchen. He didn't switch on the main light, and the glow from the candle—the flame wavering now because her hand wasn't in the least steady—somehow made him look even taller and more intimidating. Its soft glow accentuated the dark planes of his face, highlighted the perfect bone-structure, but hid the expression in his eyes.

Philippa found herself fervently wishing that he *had* been a ghost. She could probably have coped better with that! Now, instead of being cold with fright, she was hot and flustered. And her stomach had begun that ridiculous churning again, as if she were a schoolgirl who had just come face to face with her idol.

Don't be an idiot! she ordered herself with fresh determination. And do stop behaving like this every time you set eyes on this man. You don't even like him!

How can you dislike someone with such beautiful eyes, such a perfect mouth? murmured a treacherous voice inside her head. Someone whose kisses you remember for hours afterwards.

Philippa immediately clamped down on those thoughts. No, no, *no*. You're not really thinking all those things, she tried to reassure herself a little frantically. You're just tired, and it's been a crazy day. That long flight from Tunisia, your first sight of Sherringborne Manor, that awful dinner with the Dowager Countess, and then that scene with James—it's no wonder that you're feeling mixed up.

But then James came even closer, and her heart didn't just thump, it seemed to turn right over.

He came to a halt when he was just a couple of feet away. Philippa gave a small gulp, and stood very still.

'How did you know I was here?' she asked in a quavery voice.

'You triggered a couple of the internal alarms when you came creeping down.'

'Internal alarms? I didn't see or hear them.'

'Of course you didn't. They're silent alarms. If there are burglars in the house, we want to catch them.'

Philippa decided that *she* certainly wouldn't want to be a burglar who had been caught with a sackful of the Haverford family treasures slung over his shoulder! She wasn't at all sure that James would bother with the law. He might deal out a little rough justice of his own.

'If I had been a burglar, I would have had plenty of time to get clean away,' she pointed out, trying to cover up the fact that she was still shaking from his sudden appearance. 'I've been down here for at least half an hour—plenty of time to find the family jewels and make off with them!'

'I wouldn't recommend that you ever try anything like that,' he warned softly.

Philippa immediately bristled. 'I was only joking! I'm not a thief! And I never have been.'

'I didn't accuse you of theft.'

He was right, of course, and she began to feel slightly sheepish. 'As a matter of fact, I have pinched a couple of slices of bread and some cold meat,' she admitted. 'But I didn't think anyone would mind.' Then she remembered the extravagantly stocked larder. 'Why have you got so *much* food?' she asked curiously.

'The west wing of the house is almost completely self-contained, and it's often used for business conferences, meetings between heads of industries, and sometimes by government officials who want discreet, private discussions with their foreign counterparts. The cost of running and maintaining a house this size is frighteningly high; it makes sense to put part of the house to work, to help cover some of the costs.'

'Have you ever thought of opening it to the public?'

'No,' James said at once. 'This is my home.'

Philippa could appreciate that. 'If I lived here, *I* wouldn't want crowds of people thronging through every day,' she admitted. 'I think the house is absolutely beautiful. I'd like to see it always stay exactly the way it is, right now.'

'Some things have to change. If the house were still in its original state, we'd have very little heating, very primitive plumbing, and a great deal of damp and rot,' James said drily.

'Oh, you know what I mean. When Richardson drove me here from the airport, I really couldn't believe it when he said you had a butler and footmen, and you were the lord of the manor. It all sounded positively medieval! And I certainly didn't approve. But now I'm here everything seems—well, just right,' she said, trying hard to find the appropriate words. 'Sherringborne seems to be like a small, self-contained world of its own.'

'Yes, it is,' he agreed, his gaze locking on to her thoughtfully. 'I didn't expect you to appreciate that so quickly—if ever.'

She gave a sudden grin. 'You see, I'm not a complete barbarian! If Sherringborne belonged to me, I wouldn't rip everything out and fill the house with fitted carpets, ultra-modern furniture and pop art!'

'But Sherringborne never will belong to you, will it?' he said with a sudden hardening of his eyes. 'Not even if you marry Jonathan.'

Philippa gave a resigned sigh. She could never say—or do—anything right, as far as this man was concerned. Somehow he always turned it against her.

'Believe it or not, I'm not interested in owning Sherringborne,' she told him.

'No, I don't believe it,' James said grimly. 'I think that you're out for absolutely everything you can get.'

'It's too late and I'm too tired to go through all this again,' she said, half turning away from him.

He caught hold of her shoulder and swung her back to face him. 'What did Jonathan promise you? A title? This house? All the money you could ever want to spend? My nephew will have a lot of problems keeping those promises,' he warned.

Philippa glared back at him. 'Believe it or not, Jonathan never promised me anything except love. And that was all I ever wanted from him!'

James threw back his head and laughed cynically.

'Don't *do* that,' she said furiously.

'Why not? I haven't been so amused for ages.' Then the blue of his eyes abruptly turned to ice and all trace of laughter disappeared from his face. 'Do you really expect me to believe that you're a little orphan just looking for love and a family to replace the one you lost?'

'Oh, you are so hateful,' Philippa said in a choked voice.

'Just realistic,' James said coolly. 'And I understand you so well, because we're alike in many ways.'

'*Alike*?' she repeated in pure disbelief.

'If we see something we want, we go straight after it. And we get it.'

'You're talking about Jonathan again, aren't you?' she accused. 'You're accusing me of deliberately chasing after him.'

'Of course I am. And I can even understand why you did it. You've probably had a hard time since your parents died; it's never easy for a girl on her own. Jonathan was your meal ticket to an easier life.'

'I'm not that ruthless,' Philippa denied fiercely, determined not to let him see how much it hurt that he could even *think* she would ever use someone like that. Especially Jonathan, who was so nice. 'But you obviously are. What did *you* want and go after?' she challenged him with fresh boldness.

James gave an unexpected smile, but it didn't lighten the grimness of his face in any way. 'This house, of course. When my father died, the death duties and taxes threatened to bankrupt the family. Everyone said that Sherringborne Manor would have to be sold. I had to threaten, scheme, manipulate the finances, even bend the law a little, in order to keep it.'

Philippa hadn't expected to hear anything like that and she found herself unexpectedly fascinated by his admission. 'You really wanted it that much?'

'Of course. It was my inheritance.'

'I thought you were very wealthy——'

'I probably am, by normal standards. But a house this size swallows up money. You said that everything here still seems medieval in many ways, but you're wrong. An estate of this size can only survive if it's run with ultra-efficiency. The house, the farms, the various connected businesses are all run with the help of modern equipment and computers. The family investments have to be managed so that they give the maximum return. The rich can't afford to be idle any more, or they risk waking up one morning and finding that they've lost everything overnight. And they wouldn't be the only losers. All the people they employ, people who rely on them to provide decent jobs with adequate wages, would go down with them. Owning a house like this and all the land that goes with it is a huge responsibility, and one that never ends.'

His voice was deeply passionate as he spoke, and his eyes glowed with an inner light. This was obviously something that he felt extremely strongly about. Philippa's own eyes opened wide; she was completely intrigued by this new side of him that he had just revealed. She had almost forgotten how angry she had been just minutes ago, when he had made all those outrageous accusations over her relationship with Jonathan.

But James certainly hadn't forgotten anything at all. He took a step further forward, standing so close now that Philippa could feel the heat radiating from his body. She thought that she could even hear the strong, rhythmic beating of his heart.

'You should always remember that I'm successful because I don't play by the rules,' he said, his voice soft now, but with no trace of gentleness in it. 'And that it's very dangerous to make me want something that I shouldn't have, because I might just take it anyway.'

The candle flickered, almost plunging the kitchen into complete darkness. Philippa felt all her nerves tensely contract; then, to her intense relief, the flame flared again and burned brightly. It meant that she could clearly see James's face, though, and she realised at once that she had been right to feel so very nervous. Anger and desire were written in a volatile mixture over his dark features, and he seemed to be making little effort to control either. Or perhaps he couldn't.

She licked her dry lips and told herself that she had to back away, turn, run—if only her legs would move!

James's gaze locked on to the small movement of her tongue as it moistened her mouth.

'A clever little trick,' he murmured in a voice that had noticeably thickened. 'How often do you play it?'

'I never play tricks,' she said at once, although without any hope of being believed.

'Of course you do. All women do. And in the right place and at the right time they can be very enjoyable.'

There was a purely sensual note in his voice now, and she was alarmed to find herself responding to it. At the same time she was rather frantically trying to work out what he was doing. What game he was playing. And what was *she* doing, just standing here and making no effort to stop him?

James looked at her thoughtfully. 'Did you know about the burglar alarm?' he said speculatively. 'Was that another trick? Did you set it off deliberately, to make me come down here? And what about the candlelight? Very romantic, a clever feminine touch. It sets the scene perfectly.'

'I'm not that calculating,' she protested. 'I used a candle because I didn't want to switch on the main lights and disturb everyone.'

'And who is "everyone"? I'm the only other person in the house. The staff who live in have their own private quarters at the back.'

She stood very still. 'You're—you're the only one here?'

James smiled gently, and every hair on her body stood up on end as she saw the beautiful, wicked line of his mouth.

'You knew that.'

'I didn't,' she denied at once.

His fingertips brushed against her lips. 'Such a pretty mouth shouldn't tell lies. Pretty mouth,' he murmured again, staring at it so hard that Philippa could feel her lips gently quivering under that intense scrutiny. At the same time, his hand carelessly hooked a long, silky strand of her hair over his long, clever fingers.

She knew at once that she ought to wrench herself free. This man despised her, she was sure of it. She shouldn't let him touch one single hair on her head.

But the awful thing was that she *liked* his touch. She *liked* to hear him talk about her mouth.

He was close now, very close. Her heart felt as if it had stopped beating. She frantically told herself again that she had to back away, but her feet seemed glued to the floor; those brilliant blue eyes had hypnotised her, the soft rhythms of his voice had turned her limbs to jelly. This was really frightening. What on earth was happening to her?

She watched with dreadful fascination as James's mouth moved nearer. He was going to kiss her, she was absolutely certain of it, and she couldn't do a thing to stop it, which was perfectly ridiculous since she was a grown woman with a mind of her own.

But he seemed caught up in the same shameful lack of control; she could tell from the burning light in his eyes that he was angry at what was happening, but he was driven on by the desire to feel the touch of her mouth against his just one more time.

Then his mouth actually touched hers, and Philippa instantly forgot absolutely everything as a dark heat seemed to swallow her up. It was a kiss that wiped out resistance, memory, the ability to do anything except melt into complete submissiveness. A moment ago she had told herself she was a grown woman. Now she knew that she wasn't grown-up at all. No one could be completely adult until they had experienced a kiss like this!

James's mouth continued to move with deadly expertise, searching out all the small, vulnerable pleasure-spots and then provoking them into fresh flares of pure heat. The kiss went on and on until she felt dizzy and disorientated, but she didn't want it to stop; she didn't *ever* want it to stop. Then his hand touched just the very tip of her breast, and her entire body immediately jumped, as if she had received a sudden electric shock.

He moved again, more quickly, taking advantage of her surprise and lack of resistance. His fingers swiftly unfastened the buttons on her shirt, slid inside, found soft flesh which instantly burned under his touch.

Philippa gasped for breath, and frantically tried to force herself back to reality. James wouldn't allow it, though; he seemed to take a purely sensual pleasure in relentlessly pushing her further and further down into an engulfing pool of wicked delight. She was terrified of drowning in it, terrified by the way that she so easily gave up the attempt to clamber out.

Another kiss, dark and intense, sent every one of her senses reeling. His hand slowly caressed in exquisitely gentle movements, and a sweet ache spread out from the centre of her breast right through her body. She could feel the heat pouring off his own skin, and knew that everything was rocketing completely out of control; she guessed that he had never meant to go any further than that one punishing kiss.

Philippa knew that every single thing that was happening was completely wrong, but she couldn't *stop* it; she didn't seem to have any will-power left at all. The darkness of the night, the flickering candlelight, the atmosphere of the old house made it all seem almost dream-like. Her head was softly spinning. She didn't even feel like herself any more. The old Philippa had certainly never experienced anything like this!

James abandoned his searing exploration of her mouth and she heard the frustrated murmur of his voice in her ear.

'Guilt and pleasure—one feeds on the other. And now we both know how it feels, don't we? But that doesn't stop me wanting to touch every inch of you. Every secret place, where you've always wanted to be touched but never dared ask. But you'll ask me.' His finger rubbed lightly against the very tip of her breast, and it was so pleasurable that it *hurt*. 'I can make you ask, can't I, Philippa?' he challenged her, his voice harsh with a mixture of triumph and self-disgust.

CHAPTER FIVE

PHILIPPA desperately wanted to lie, wanted to shout out, *No*. Her tongue wouldn't twist itself round that simple word, though, and while she was still fighting to speak—even to breathe—James's hand began to move again with deadly precision.

She had known all along that this man was dangerous. Only she hadn't realised *how* dangerous. He could whip her breath away with the touch of his hand, make her heart almost stop beating with one burning glance from those impossibly blue eyes.

His fingers slid over her skin, and Philippa's world instantly went completely haywire. The gentleness had gone; this time he touched her swiftly and purposefully, moving from her aching breasts to the convulsively contracting muscles of her stomach, sliding beneath the soft material of her skirt, pausing only to destroy, with one brief, hard kiss, the small sound of protest that escaped her. Then he relentlessly moved on, his hands swooping lower and lower, until he held the most vulnerable pleasure-spots of her body cupped against the hot palm of his hand.

Philippa was devastated by a completely new kind of pleasure, and pole-axed by the discovery that she wanted even more. She knew that she ought to be terrified by this power he had over her—this was the *Earl of Sherringborne*, she reminded herself, with a deep convulsive shiver. But it was hard to remember that, hard even to care, while her body melted with these utterly delicious sensations.

The dark shadows of the kitchen made it seem even more intimate; she found herself digging her fingers deeply into James's hard muscles, and then heard the breath swiftly escape from his lungs, as if he had been hit by a strong and unexpected wave of pleasure. She loved that. Loved it in a way that really scared her. She wanted to do it again, and only just managed to stop herself.

Don't let this go any further, she warned herself. Inexperienced though she was, she knew instinctively how near the edge he was. If he lost control completely——

She was quite sure, without knowing how, that this was a new kind of situation for James, too. A sudden flush of excitement rushed through her. What would it be like if he *did* lose control? If she could make him?

Don't even think about it! she warned herself in pure alarm. Only someone who was quite mad would try something like that. The only trouble was, she felt a little mad tonight.

James pulled away from her and his eyes locked on to her face. 'What are you thinking?' he demanded, with unnerving perception.

Philippa didn't dare tell him. 'N-nothing,' she lied.

'Yes, you are,' he growled, shaking her lightly. 'I can feel it in your body. See it in your eyes. Tell me!'

But she was suddenly terrified of where this was leading. 'If you must know, I was thinking that I really don't like you at all,' she lied again, desperate now to lead him away from the truth.

He smiled then, a smile that made her skin prickle and then burn.

'We don't need to like each other. The problem is that we do like *this*.'

Another intense kiss left her mouth bruised, but it was the sweetest kind of bruising she had ever experienced. Then she began to panic as she realised that she wanted her whole body to feel just as crushed and invaded. That really is insane, she thought incredulously, but she still couldn't get rid of that secret, shameful longing. And what if James found out about it? What if he already *knew*?

Philippa shivered convulsively from head to toe. She knew that she had never been in such a dangerous situation in her entire life.

Every one of her senses was so heightened now that she could smell his desire, a totally male scent, and she knew that her own body must be giving off the same betraying signals. Whatever James's reasons for starting this, she knew that it had escalated into something that both of them were finding almost impossible to control. She realised that her palms were pressing hard against his powerful chest, but not to push him away. Instead they registered with ashamed pleasure the fast, heavy beat of his heart and the fresh tension in his muscles.

He moved against her quite deliberately, forcing her to be aware of the aroused state of his body, the heat that was beginning to pour off him, the irregularity of his breathing. But almost instantly he moved away again, denying himself further contact, as if to punish himself for wanting something that he knew he shouldn't have.

And he punished her as well, deliberately exploring every inch of her until she wanted to scream with frustration as his fingers rasped almost roughly against her painfully sensitive skin, but without making any effort to alleviate the desire that he was so deliberately arousing.

Sometimes he would only touch her through her clothes, which was even worse because it meant that he was denying both of them the intense pleasure of skin-to-skin contact.

Philippa could feel the anger in his touch, anger directed at himself as much as at her. But he didn't stop. And, overwhelmed and feeling frighteningly lost, she didn't try to pull away.

Then the kitchen was suddenly plunged into darkness as the candle-flame guttered and died. They both stood absolutely motionless for a few moments. Philippa was aware of a deep sense of shock. In the absolute darkness she felt even more vulnerable, and she wrapped her arms around her body as if to protect herself.

James muttered something hoarsely under his breath. An instant later he wheeled away from her, strode over to the door and slammed down the light switch.

As the bright electric glare from the fluorescent lights overhead flooded the kitchen, they stared at each other in the revealing brilliance. James's face was formidably fierce, and marked with a deep flush of colour across his cheekbones. Philippa knew that, by contrast, she had gone desperately pale. She just didn't understand what had happened between them tonight; didn't even think that she *wanted* to understand it.

'You shouldn't have done any of that,' she somehow managed to get out at last in a totally shaken voice. 'You shouldn't even have touched me.'

'Do you think I don't know that?' James demanded harshly. 'But I didn't hear you object. I didn't feel you trying to push me away. And we both know why, don't we?'

What was he talking about now? Her head was still whirling around too much for her to work it out.

'You seem to have lost what little interest you ever had in Jonathan since you came to Sherringborne,' he went on tersely. 'Why is that, Philippa? Have you seen how much else there is on offer, and decided to go for it? I think that you're greedy enough. And sufficiently lacking in morals!'

His cruel and unjustified attack felt almost like a physical blow. She visibly flinched. Then she took refuge in anger.

'And what about *you*? Jonathan's your nephew!' she reminded him bluntly. 'Or perhaps you behave like this with all his girlfriends,' she accused, just wanting to hit back at him in any way she could.

James took two quick strides towards her. Then he swiftly checked himself. 'No, I don't think I'd better touch you again tonight,' he said in a voice that was thick with rage. 'Because I don't think that you'd like it as much as you did earlier!'

'Oh, why stop now?' she challenged him with pure recklessness. 'After all, we're the perfect couple, aren't we? I'm meant to want you because of your money and title. And you want me because—well, why *do* you want me, James?' she said, her brown eyes staring boldly into his.

'Perhaps I'm interested in seeing just how far you'll go to get what you want,' he said in a cold voice.

'No, I don't think so,' Philippa said, amazed that her nerve was holding out long enough to let her stand up to him like this.

'Then maybe I want to find out everything about you. And this is a quick and easy way of doing it.'

If anyone else had said that to her—especially after what had just happened—Philippa might have thought the words were meant lovingly. That he really wanted to know more about her. Where James Haverford was concerned, though, she knew better, and she swiftly shook her head.

'You're not interested in me.'

'But I certainly am,' James told her, and his voice had altered now; it was much softer, but there was an edged quality to it that made her suddenly shiver. He had taken another step closer, and he was standing very close again, close enough for her to smell the fresh scent of his skin, feel his warmth. A sudden urge to touch him swept over Philippa, completely horrifying her. How could she want to do something like that, when he was looking at her with something very like hatred?

'When I know all about you, I'll know exactly how to protect Jonathan from you,' he went on. 'And I've learnt a lot tonight. I think that you know just how much.'

'You don't know anything about me at all,' she told him in a voice that had begun to tremble.

He lifted his hand and let his fingers run lightly over the nape of her neck. Heat instantly rushed to her skin where he had touched it, staining it with betraying colour.

'Of course I do,' he said. He forced his hand to move away from her again, although it seemed to take a great deal of will-power. 'And I intend to learn much more,' he warned. 'By the time I'm through, you won't have any secrets from me, Philippa.'

She desperately hoped that he would never find out how he could toss her straight back into total confusion just by saying her name. That was one secret she wanted to take with her to the grave!

He stared at her hard for a few more moments. For a heart-stopping instant she thought that he was going to kiss her again.

James's vivid blue eyes instantly hardened. 'Oh, no,' he said, reading her thoughts with an ease that filled her with pure alarm. 'No more. Enough damage has been done tonight.'

'Not just by me,' she said defensively.

'No, not just by you,' he agreed in a grim voice. His gaze bored into her. 'Bringing you to Sherringborne was a big mistake, wasn't it?' he stated tautly. Then he turned round and swiftly left the kitchen.

Philippa could hear his footsteps echoing away in the distance until there was nothing left except silence. A silence broken only by her own fractured breathing and the violent pounding of her heart.

Dangerous, dangerous, *dangerous*. The word repeated itself over and over inside her head, in rhythm with her beating heart. Everything inside her seemed mixed up, every emotion turned inside out. And she was ashamed to admit that there had been something about the confrontation that made her feel vital and alive. Her skin still burned with a strange flush of excitement.

'This has all got to stop,' she whispered to herself. 'And right now. Before it's too late!'

Too late for what? Philippa decided to be a total coward and not even try to answer that question.

Although she had never expected to sleep well on her first night at Sherringborne Manor, Philippa hadn't expected to toss and turn until dawn. Her body refused to relax and her mind raced all night. She felt totally over-stimulated, and confused thoughts rushed round and round inside her head until it began to ache with sheer tension.

Then there was the sense of guilt which swept over her in huge waves. Her engagement to Jonathan was only unofficial, but it *was* a commitment. She shouldn't even be thinking about another man—let alone letting him kiss her. And do all those other things to her!

She tried to convince herself that it hadn't been her fault—James had simply overwhelmed her—but that didn't work. Philippa was always very honest with herself. She *had* had chances to get away, to put a stop to the situation before everything had got completely out of hand—but she hadn't taken them. She gave a small groan and pulled the covers up over her head, as if trying to hide from herself. She couldn't blot out what had happened, though, and she certainly couldn't come up with any acceptable excuses for the way she had behaved.

Then another thought struck her like a thunderbolt, making her suddenly sit upright. What if James told Jonathan what had happened tonight? Just the thought of it made Philippa go completely cold. She couldn't bear to see Jonathan hurt; she was so very fond of him.

'James wouldn't do that,' she whispered to herself. 'It would mean admitting how badly *he* had behaved. It might even mean that Jonathan would end up hating him, as well as me.'

But she suspected that James would do whatever had to be done to put a stop to her marriage to Jonathan, even if it was at a terrible cost to himself.

Philippa desperately wished that Jonathan would come home straight away. Perhaps if she could see him, talk to him she would be able to resolve all the doubts that were swirling round inside her own mind.

She finally managed to sleep for a couple of hours just as the sky began to lighten. She was woken up again by the sound of loud birdsong right outside her window, and the bright blaze of early morning sunshine.

She huddled under the sheets for a while longer, putting off the moment when she would have to face the new day, and all the problems it was bound to bring. Then she gave a small sigh, forced herself out of bed and padded over to the window.

Her room was at the back of the house, with breath-taking views of the grounds beyond. The gardens below were divided into small, enclosed areas, like a series of outdoor rooms. Beneath her window was the walled garden, with flowers spilling over on to gravelled paths. Clematis, climbing roses and honeysuckle covered the mellow brick walls, pinks and sweet-william added to the perfume softly drifting up, and brightly coloured spikes of lupins and brilliant blue spires of delphiniums shot up at the back of the borders. Philippa forced herself to look away from the delphiniums. Their colour reminded her too vividly of James's eyes. Instead she let her gaze roam over the brilliant red patches of poppies that dazzled in the sunshine, and the tall daises in white and cream and yellow that were just beginning to open.

An open archway at the far end led into a circular area which had a large pond and fountain as its centrepiece. The water was fringed with the large, glossy, patterned leaves of hostas, and muted flashes of colour glinted in the pond as great koi carp lazily swam just below the surface.

Beyond a row of dark, clipped yews was the rose garden, linked by stone steps to a sunken area planted with azaleas and rhododendrons, which would be a brilliant riot of colour in early spring. Paths led off through half-hidden archways to other areas of the garden, and Philippa could catch distant glimpses of a stream and miniature waterfall, exotic trees, weathered statues, and great stone urns full of tumbling geraniums and elegantly arching fuchsias.

For a few moments she almost forgot about last night. She was enchanted by the garden, and wished that she could look at it every morning for the rest of her life.

You could, if you married Jonathan, murmured a small voice inside her head. Sherringborne Manor doesn't belong to him, but it's his home. You could persuade him to live here. You could probably persuade him to do almost anything.

Philippa firmly pushed that thought right out of her head, though. She wouldn't use Jonathan—wouldn't use anyone—in such a cynical way. When she married, it would be for love. The only trouble was, she wasn't quite so certain any more that she knew what love was. When she had first met Jonathan, she had been fairly sure. Now, with every day that passed, she became less sure about—well, about everything!

She knew that part of her *had* already fallen in love, though—with this house. It had fascinated and captivated her from the moment she had first seen it, and she understood completely why James had gone to such lengths to keep it after the death of his father.

There—she had said James's name again! And nothing dreadful had happened. The sky hadn't fallen in or the world crashed around her. Perhaps she was finally learning to cope with the Earl of Sherringborne! Then Philippa gave a small sigh. She had to be truthful and admit that she wasn't coping at all. If she was going to get through the rest of her stay here at Sherringborne, she had to lay down some very firm ground rules. And the first—and most important!—was never to let James kiss her or touch her again.

Philippa repeated that a second time, as if she needed to get it fixed very firmly inside her head. Then she showered, dressed, left her room and walked firmly downstairs.

In a few moments she would be facing James over the breakfast-table. That would be hard, but she had to do it. She *would* do it, she told herself staunchly. And she wouldn't even think about last night, or those kisses, or everything else that had happened between them.

She had to say that twice, as well. She was just about to repeat it for a third time when a nearby door opened and a dark-haired woman came bustling out.

'Miss Martin?' she said briskly. 'I'm Mrs Evans, the housekeeper. Are you ready for breakfast? Come this way,' she said, without even giving Philippa a chance to answer her question.

Philippa found herself being led at a fast trot past the entrance to the Great Hall, and into a smaller room at the back of the house. She relaxed slightly when she saw there was no one else in the room. A table was laid, and a heated trolley stood to one side filled with covered dishes.

'We serve plain food in this house, unless it's a special occasion,' Mrs Evans told her in the same brisk tone. 'If you have any special dietary requirements, please let Mrs Williams, the cook, know, and she'll prepare something appropriate.'

'Plain food is fine,' Philippa said, rather bowled over by all this super-efficiency first thing in the morning. 'Er—am I the first one down to breakfast?' she asked cautiously.

'No, the last,' Mrs Evans replied, with a slight note of censure in her voice. 'His Lordship is always up early.

He's already eaten and gone out. We've kept some food warm for you, though.'

'I'm sorry if I'm late,' she said apologetically.

'You haven't been here long enough to learn the routine of the household,' Mrs Evans replied. Then she hurried off. She was obviously a woman who didn't believe in wasting a single minute of time.

Once she had gone, Philippa lifted the lids off the covered dishes and looked appreciatively at the beautifully prepared eggs, the crisp, perfect bacon, the golden toast. She piled her plate high with food, and then ate with relish. It made her feel even more relaxed to know that James wouldn't be walking through the door at any moment.

She had pushed away her empty plate and was just pouring herself a second cup of coffee when the door suddenly opened. Philippa's hand instantly shook and she nearly spilt coffee all over the tablecloth. Then her hand quickly steadied again as she saw a young girl walking into the room, not James.

She was maybe thirteen or fourteen, thin and tall, with good features that were half hidden under too much inexpertly applied make up. Her dark hair was cut into a spiky style, she wore cropped skin-tight leggings and a faded sweatshirt, and she was scowling unattractively. When she saw Philippa, the scowl deepened.

'Who are you?' she demanded.

'Philippa Martin,' she said, trying to keep her own voice pleasant. Privately she wondered if *anyone* in this house was ever going to give her a friendly greeting.

'Philippa who?' said the girl rudely. Then she gave an irritable toss of her head. 'Oh, yes, I know who you are. You're engaged to my brother.'

Philippa realised then that this had to be Stephanie, Jonathan's sister. But she certainly wasn't anything like him! Philippa had expected a younger version of Jonathan, a girl who was carelessly good-looking and charming, not this prickly, hostile teenager who seemed to be deliberately downplaying the looks that she had. And she was certainly short on charm!

She hid her surprise and made an effort to keep her own voice warm. 'I'm pleased that we've had a chance to meet, Stephanie.'

Stephanie stared straight back at her with eyes that were golden-brown, instead of the usual disconcertingly intense Haverford blue. They certainly weren't friendly eyes, though.

'Don't bother trying to be nice to me,' she said bluntly. 'We're not going to be friends.'

Philippa checked the retort that sprang to her own tongue. Perhaps Stephanie was just having a bad morning, she told herself. Or she was in one of the black moods that teenagers were notorious for.

'How can you be certain that we won't be friends, when you don't even know me?' she asked levelly instead.

'I don't want to know you.' Stephanie picked up a piece of toast and nibbled at it. 'What's the point, when you're not even going to be here for very long? Uncle James says that he's going to stop you marrying my brother,' she said with obvious satisfaction. 'I heard him talking to my grandmother about you. They both think that you're not at all suitable.'

'Do they?' Philippa said, the colour rising dangerously in her face. 'Don't you think that *I* should decide who I marry?'

'Uncle James makes all the important decisions around here,' Stephanie said, with an unexpected touch of pride.

AND YOU COULD GET FREE BOOKS, A FREE CRYSTAL NECKLACE AND A SURPRISE GIFT!

NO COST! NO OBLIGATION TO BUY!
NO PURCHASE NECESSARY!

PLAY "LUCKY 7"
AND GET AS MANY AS SIX FREE GIFTS...

HOW TO PLAY:

1 With a coin, carefully scratch away the silver panel opposite. Then check the claim chart to see what we have for you - FREE BOOKS and gifts - ALL YOURS! ALL FREE!

2 When you return this card we'll send you specially selected Mills & Boon romances and the gifts you qualify for, absolutely FREE. There's no catch. You're under no obligation to buy anything. We charge nothing for your first shipment. And you don't have to make any minimum number of purchases.

3 After you've received your FREE books, if we don't hear from you, we will send you six brand new Mills & Boon romances to read and enjoy every month for just £1.99* each - the same price as the books in the shops. There is no extra charge for postage and packing and no hidden extras.

4 The fact is thousands of readers enjoy receiving books through the post from the Reader Service. They like the convenience of home delivery... they like getting the best new novels at least a month before they're available in the shops... and they love their subscriber Newsletter, featuring author news, horoscopes, penfriends, competitions and much more.

5 We hope that after receiving your free books you'll want to remain a subscriber. But the choice is yours - to continue or cancel, anytime at all! So why not take up our invitation - you'll be glad you did!

*Prices subject to change without notice.

You'll look like a million dollars when you wear this lovely necklace! Its cobra-link chain is a generous 18" long, and the multi-faceted Austrian crystal sparkles like a diamond!

NOT ACTUAL SIZE

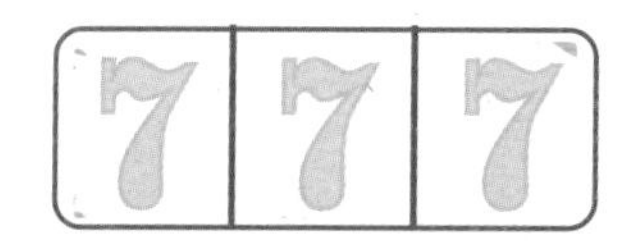

Play "Lucky 7"

Just scratch away the silver panel with a coin.
Then check below to see how many FREE GIFTS will be yours.

YES! I have scratched away the silver panel. Please send me all the gifts for which I qualify. I understand that I am under no obligation to purchase any books, as explained on the opposite page. I am over 18 years of age.

MS/MRS/MISS/MR 5A5R

ADDRESS

POSTCODE

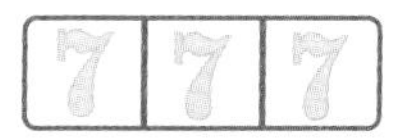

WORTH FOUR FREE BOOKS
PLUS A NECKLACE AND MYSTERY GIFT

WORTH FOUR FREE BOOKS
PLUS A MYSTERY GIFT

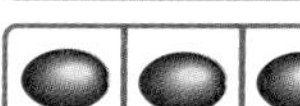

WORTH FOUR FREE BOOKS

WORTH TWO FREE BOOKS

Offer expires 30th November 1995. We reserve the right to refuse an application. *Prices and terms subject to change without notice. Offer only valid in UK and Eire and not available to current subscribers to this series. Overseas readers please write for details. Southern Africa write to: IBS, Private Bag X3010, Randburg 2125.
You may be mailed with offers from other reputable companies as a result of this application. If you would rather not receive such offers, please tick box. ☐

mps MAILING PREFERENCE SERVICE

READER SERVICE 'NO RISK' GUARANTEE

- You're not required to buy a single book!
- You must be completely satisfied or you may cancel at any time simply by writing to us. You will receive no more books; you'll have no further obligation.
- The free books and gifts you receive from this offer remain yours to keep no matter what you decide.

HARLEQUIN MILLS & BOON
FREEPOST
P.O. Box 70
Croydon
Surrey
CR9 9EL

NO
STAMP
NEEDED

She clearly had a great deal of respect for her uncle. 'And it's no use trying to fight him,' she added. 'You won't win. No one ever does.'

'Thanks for the advice, but I don't need it. Your uncle might be the lord of the manor and control everything around here, but he isn't going to run *my* life!'

Stephanie simply shrugged. She obviously thought that Philippa was pretty stupid even to think about taking on James.

Philippa decided that this wasn't a good start to her relationship with Stephanie, and forced herself to calm down. Getting into an argument with her would be the very worst thing she could do. Instead she ought to be trying to make a friend of this girl. She was, after all, Jonathan's sister, and it might not even be her fault that she had been so rude. She was only repeating what her uncle had said.

'Look, we seem to have got off to a bad start. Why don't you sit down and have some breakfast?' she invited. 'Perhaps we could talk, and get a few things straightened out.'

'There's nothing to talk about,' Stephanie said, the old hostility returning to her voice. 'And I've already eaten. But even if I hadn't I wouldn't need your permission to sit down and have breakfast. This is *my* home, and I'll do whatever I want to do in it.'

'I'm sure that you always do exactly what you want. But I don't think it would hurt you to make an effort at least to be polite,' Philippa retorted, finally goaded into retaliation.

Stephanie glared back at her and was obviously about to make an even ruder retort, but she was interrupted by the opening of the door.

Both of them swung round as James came into the room. He was dressed very casually this morning in jeans and a sweatshirt, but there was certainly nothing casual about his attitude. His blue gaze went first to his niece's defiant eyes and then to Philippa's flushed skin. Then he gave a dark frown.

'What's going on here?' he demanded curtly.

'I came down to breakfast, but *she* was here first,' Stephanie jumped in quickly. 'I don't like her, Uncle James,' she added, giving a small and very convincing sniff, as if she were actually near to tears. 'She hasn't been at all nice to me.'

Philippa's brown eyes immediately flew wide open. OK, so they hadn't become best friends at first sight, but she hadn't said anything unkind. In fact she had hardly raised her voice to the girl. She thought that she had actually been very restrained. Most other people would have given Stephanie a stern lecture on manners!

James's face had darkened still further. 'I want to know exactly what's happened between the two of you,' he said, his gaze fixing on Philippa.

'Nothing's happened,' Philippa said at once. She was annoyed to hear an almost apologetic note in her voice. Why should she be apologetic when she hadn't done anything wrong?

From the hard expression on his face, he obviously didn't believe her. Stephanie went over to her uncle and clung on to his arm, obviously determined to make her story even more convincing.

'She isn't going to stay here, is she?' she said in a soft little voice quite unlike the antagonistic tone she had used to Philippa. 'I really don't want her here.'

'Oh, for heaven's sake!' Philippa exploded in complete exasperation. 'She's behaving as if I'm some kind of monster. This really is getting quite ridiculous!'

James was still looking at her suspiciously, though, and he had put his arm protectively around his niece's shoulder. 'Tell me exactly what you did,' he ordered.

Philippa really couldn't believe this was happening. 'I didn't do anything,' she defended herself. 'Except put up with a lot of insults!'

But the two Haverford faces stared back at her, both of them equally hostile now, and she could feel herself beginning to feel intimidated. Two against one. It wasn't fair!

She had known from the very beginning how formidable James Haverford could be. She hadn't expected his young niece to be almost as alarming!

Pull yourself together, she instructed herself sternly. Don't let them get to you like this. Stand up for yourself!

'I'm still waiting for an explanation,' James reminded her in a warning tone. His gaze swung back to his niece. 'Stephanie?'

Stephanie began to shift a little uneasily from foot to foot. Perhaps even she balked at the thought of telling her uncle outright lies. Past experience had probably taught her that that was a very unwise thing to do.

'I just don't like her,' she muttered again at last. 'And I don't think she should stay here. Not while Jonathan's still away.'

'I invited her here. She is, after all, engaged to Jonathan,' James reminded her, although something about his tone, too carefully controlled, gave Philippa the impression that he hadn't liked saying those words.

'Oh, you know what Jonathan's like. It was probably just one of his spur-of-the-moment ideas,' Stephanie said at once. 'He's always making plans that he's completely forgotten by the next day.'

'I don't think that even Jonathan's likely to forget that he's got a fiancée,' James said drily. 'But there's no need to get upset over the situation, Stephanie. This is a big house; there's plenty of room for everyone to have their own space.'

'Are you telling Stephanie that she doesn't have to talk to me? Or even see me?' Philippa demanded. 'I don't think that's going to solve the situation.'

James's eyes fixed on her again, quelling her into silence. 'Since the situation isn't of Stephanie's making, I think she should be allowed to handle it in whatever way suits her best.'

'And, of course, if I don't have any contact with Stephanie, I won't be able to *influence* her, will I?' Philippa retorted, remembering James's previous instructions to stay away from his niece. 'Well, I'd just like to say a special thanks to all you Haverfords at this point for making me feel so very welcome and part of the family! And since you obviously won't miss me if I go out for a while, I'm going for a walk around the grounds.' She got to her feet, went over to the door, then turned back to face them. 'It's a lovely morning, and I want to explore. I think that I ought to get to know the place, don't you?' she added, with a challenging look at both of them. 'After all, once we're married Jonathan and I might decide that we want to live here.'

That remark certainly hit home. It brought the scowl straight back to Stephanie's face, and James's mouth hardened dangerously. Philippa knew that she had pushed things just a little too far, and that it was time to leave. She quickly left the room before either of them could take up her challenge. She didn't think that she could cope this morning with Stephanie *and* James's infamous temper!

Once she was outside, her nerve finally collapsed. When she reached the garden, she had to sit down for a few minutes, until she had stopped shaking.

She found herself fervently wishing that she had someone she could talk to about this. If only Jonathan were here. She would give anything to see a friendly face!

It was at times like this that she really missed having a family. Yes, she had friends, good friends, but they just weren't the same as a parent, a sister or a brother. Someone who had known her all her life.

Philippa took a deep breath. 'Come on,' she whispered to herself, 'this is the wrong time to start feeling vulnerable. You've been on your own since you were eighteen; you should have learnt to deal with it by now. And even when you did have a family, things weren't that good. Too much stifling love can be as bad as too little.'

She gave a small sigh. Her life had never been particularly easy, but just when she had thought she was coping with it quite well James Haverford had come along and knocked everything completely off course!

She wondered if she should just give up, run away from Sherringborne. But Philippa wasn't a quitter, and with fresh determination she told herself that she *wouldn't* let these Haverfords beat her.

All the same, the next few days were hard. Stephanie followed her uncle's advice and kept well out of Philippa's way, but James was around for much of the time. Philippa was edgily aware of him watching her, as if waiting for her to do or say something wrong. And she felt uncomfortable, having so little to occupy her time. She was used to a busy life, somehow fitting in her own washing, cooking, shopping and cleaning. Here, there were staff to do everything. She literally had nothing to do. She spent a couple of hours each day exercising, to keep her body supple and tuned up. Dancers who allowed their bodies to get stiff and out of condition were dropped very early from auditions! For much of the rest of the time she explored the house and grounds, making new discoveries all the time and finding secret corners that delighted her. And she began to haunt the extensive library, hunting out old books as she delved deeper and deeper into the fascinating history of Sherringborne.

She and James usually had their evening meal together, and, by keeping the conversation carefully neutral, Philippa managed to avoid any more major confrontations. One safe topic was Sherringborne; she found that James was an absolute mine of information and he didn't seem to mind talking about it.

'Has anyone ever written a history of your family?' she asked one evening as they finished their meal with coffee.

'Not recently,' he replied.

'Someone should,' Philippa said with enthusiasm. 'It's such intriguing stuff. The Sherringbornes have served at court, fought in most of the great battles, been spies, mercenaries, priests, sea captains and even pirates. They've married famous people and had infamous affairs. One of your ancestors gambled away such a huge fortune in the eighteenth century that he nearly lost everything—the house and the entire estate. He only saved it at the last moment by getting a rich heiress to fall in love with him and marry him——' She stopped, breathless, and then suddenly gave a wry smile. 'Why am I telling you all this? You know it already.'

'Of course I do,' James agreed.

He seemed unexpectedly relaxed this evening, so she chanced another question.

'There doesn't seem to be very much about the recent history of your family, though. Just very basic information that doesn't really tell me anything.'

'All the family papers for the past few years are locked away,' he said more abruptly. 'There's no reason why anyone—and especially you—should see them.'

Philippa ignored the deliberate rebuff. She was beginning to be intrigued. 'Why?' she asked. She gave a faint grin. 'Was there some great scandal that you want to keep secret?'

'No scandal,' James said shortly. 'And nothing amusing, either,' he said, his face darkening as his gaze fixed on her smile. 'Unless you find the deaths of half the members of our family funny!'

That certainly shocked her into a very sober expression. Her eyes widened and she almost stopped breathing for a few moments.

'You're talking about Jonathan and Stephanie's parents?' she said in a voice that was very much more subdued.

'And my father,' James said starkly.

'What—what happened?' Philippa asked hesitantly.

James was looking as if he already regretted having said anything at all. She was quite sure that he wasn't going to tell her any more. Without any warning, though, he began to speak, as if he was driven by a sudden compulsion to talk about something that had been bottled up inside for far too long.

'Jonathan's parents were the first to die. My older brother and his wife——' A shadow swept over his face and his blue eyes were totally bleak. 'They went on holiday,' he said in a flat tone, as if he could only talk about it if he forced every shade of emotion from his voice. 'It was their first holiday without Jonathan and Stephanie, the first time in years that they had gone away on their own——' He abruptly stopped again. Philippa held her breath; she didn't dare say anything, didn't dare even move. She could see James's hands pressing against the table, slowly turning white with tension.

'My brother married very young,' he went on at last. 'He was just eighteen, and Justine, his wife, only seventeen. Jonathan was born just a year later, so they had to take on the responsibilities of parenthood very early. They didn't mind, though; they loved each other and adored the baby. They were thrilled when Stephanie was born, because Justine had had trouble becoming pregnant again. They never seemed to have any time to themselves, though. That was why my wedding anniversary gift to them was a holiday. I promised them I would look after Jonathan and Stephanie while they were away; all they had to do was relax and enjoy themselves for a couple of weeks.'

Philippa's heart began to thump much harder because the totally grim set of James's face warned her that something very terrible had happened. She didn't dare ask what it was, though. She just had to wait for him to finish his compulsive confession.

'Their plane went down mid-ocean,' he said at last in a harsh tone. 'No one has ever found out why. There was talk of a mid-air explosion, even the possibility of a bomb on board, but nothing's ever been proved. There was no wreckage—no bodies—no survivors——'

Philippa sat there in shocked silence, her throat very tight and dry. She fervently wished that she had never asked about his family history. She knew all too well what it was like to relive old pain. There were times even now when she couldn't bear to think about the death of her parents, even though she hadn't ever been able to feel very close to them and much of her life had been a battle to break free of their over-protectiveness. James had obviously been close to his brother, though, which must make it so much worse. And he had *sent* them on that holiday.

'I'm sorry,' she said inadequately. 'If I'd known all this, I wouldn't——'

'Wouldn't have asked about it?' James cut in, his eyes suddenly brilliantly flashing back into life. 'But if you intend to marry into this family, you have to know about it. And it's better that you hear it from me than from Jonathan. He hates talking about it; if you try he simply says that he can't even remember that time very well. He deals with it by pretending to forget it. I wish I could damned well forget it,' he said with sudden savagery, making her jump. 'But I suppose that it's a fitting punishment that I can't.'

'You can't blame yourself,' she said at once, with a huge surge of sympathy for him. 'What happened wasn't your fault.'

Anger lit his face, but it was aimed entirely at himself. 'Of course it was! They didn't want to take that holiday, they didn't want to leave their children, but *I* persuaded them. *I* knew what was best for them,' he said with a scorching sarcasm that again was self-directed. 'I booked and paid for the tickets, but what I really gave them was a death sentence! And it didn't even end there. My father never got over the loss of his eldest son. He died just six months later. In a roundabout way, I killed all three of them!'

CHAPTER SIX

A TERRIBLE silence filled the room after James had spoken those last words. He stared grimly ahead of him, and Philippa didn't dare say anything to break that silence.

She was shocked by what he had said, and amazed that he had let her catch a glimpse of his own private hell. All that guilt, seething under that arrogant façade! And she understood much better now why he was so protective towards Jonathan and Stephanie. James had promised his brother that he would look after his children while he was away, expecting it to be for just a couple of weeks. And now, years later, he was still fiercely keeping that promise.

Philippa began to look at him with new respect. She certainly admired the way that he insisted on taking responsibility for what had happened. Most people would run a mile from an awful burden like that!

She couldn't believe that he was to blame for the tragedy, though. He had been trying to *help* his brother; the rest was just a terrible twist of fate. And she definitely approved of his protective attitude towards his niece and nephew. That must have helped them get through the difficult time after their parents' death. She certainly wished that she had had someone strong and supportive around after her own parents had died.

After a few more moments, James sat back. His face and voice were locked back under control again, and his expression was quite unreadable.

'So,' he said in a very even tone, 'a few of the family skeletons have tumbled out of the closet.'

'They're not skeletons. What happened was an accident,' Philippa said with total conviction. 'A dreadful accident. Come on,' she said firmly, 'you're intelligent enough to know that it wasn't your fault.'

He smiled grimly. 'My head knows that. But something deep inside me won't acknowledge it.'

'I can understand why you feel responsible, but *no one* could foresee that something as awful as that would happen. And since then you've done everything you could for your brother's children,' Philippa reminded him. 'That's got to count for a great deal. You must have given up a large part of your own life to do that.'

'It wasn't a hard choice. And my brother would certainly have done the same for me, if the situation had been reversed. There was only a year between us in age, and we were always very close. I still miss him like hell,' he admitted with unexpected frankness.

'Of course you do. I know what it's like to lose part of your family. You never quite get over it.' She was silent for a few moments, thinking of her own mother and father. Then she asked, 'How did you cope with Jonathan and Stephanie when you were first left with them? Having them around all the time must have changed your life quite dramatically.'

She saw his eyes briefly turn hard again as the old memories flooded back into his mind.

'It certainly meant a very different lifestyle. It also meant abandoning the plans for my wedding.'

Fresh shock rushed through her. 'Wedding?' she got out in a forced voice. 'You—you were going to be married?'

'Until my bride-to-be decided that, much as she wanted a husband with a title and a stately home, she *didn't* want a ready-made family,' James said grimly.

Philippa realised that she was breathing very shallowly. Don't be so stupid, she told herself numbly. You must have known there would be women in his past. Probably lots of them! Anyway, it's nothing to do with you, so why are you reacting like this?

She didn't know, which worried her even more.

'I suppose some women feel they just can't cope with someone else's children,' she said in a low voice.

'Or they're so selfish that they don't even want to try and cope,' James said harshly. 'Apparently, even a title and a great deal of money and status weren't sufficient compensation for the disruption that Jonathan and Stephanie would cause to her social and private life, as my dear wife-to-be so succinctly put it. She kept the engagement ring, of course. She had a passion for diamonds, and she certainly didn't want to walk away with nothing.'

Philippa felt as if she was slowly beginning to understand everything so much more clearly. No wonder James was so wary of fortune-hunters when he had had first-hand experience!

She realised that she had found out more about his personal and private life this evening than during her entire stay here. From the closed expression that was settling over his face, though, he must have realised just how much he had admitted. She had the feeling that no more information was going to be forthcoming.

She expected him to get up and leave the room. Instead, however, his blue gaze fixed on her again.

'Since we seem to have strayed on to the subject of marriage, perhaps this is a good time to warn you that my mother's planning a party for you this Saturday. It's to celebrate your forthcoming marriage to Jonathan, of course.'

Philippa was well aware that he was deliberately steering the conversation away from himself, but she was so dismayed by what he had said that she didn't try to stop him.

'An engagement party?' she said, her eyebrows flying up into a worried frown.

'She doesn't approve of the engagement, of course, but she's a great believer in protocol. As Jonathan's fiancée, you have to be introduced to distant relatives and family friends. I believe she's inviting a few dozen people for drinks and a light supper.'

'A few *dozen*?' Philippa knew very well that she was repeating everything, like a parrot, but she certainly didn't want an engagement party when she was no longer sure that she even wanted to go through with the engagement!

'Jonathan is very popular,' James said, his eyes narrowing as they fixed on her face. 'People are naturally interested in meeting his fiancée.'

'But—shouldn't we wait until Jonathan comes back home?'

'Once Jonathan returns, there'll certainly be an official engagement party,' James agreed. 'This is just an informal affair, people meeting and talking over drinks.'

'Several *dozen* people,' she reminded him, biting her lip. 'Look, perhaps you could talk with your mother, persuade her to call off the party.'

'And why should I do that?' He was studying her with great intensity now, and Philippa felt even more flustered. She wouldn't—*couldn't*—explain to him her doubts about her engagement. He would demand to know why she was having doubts, and she certainly didn't want to tell him. It would mean admitting that he was the one dominating her thoughts recently, not Jonathan. Admitting a whole lot of things that she definitely didn't want him to know!

'Please, just cancel the party,' she said, hunting for some plausible excuse. 'I'm—I'm no good at that kind of social occasion.'

'The party is already planned; it's too late to cancel. And you *will* be there,' James warned. 'I won't see my mother humiliated because the guest of honour hasn't turned up.'

'Your mother doesn't even like me! Why should I worry about spoiling her party?' she said recklessly.

James got to his feet and walked round the table until he was standing directly opposite her. Philippa almost stopped breathing as he towered over her, and her hands gripped the sides of the chair so hard that they turned quite white.

'My mother might be strong-willed and opinionated, but she's also physically very frail,' he said, fixing her with his hard blue gaze. 'She had a mild stroke a couple of years ago, and I certainly don't intend that she should have another. That means that we all go out of our way to make sure she isn't subjected to any kind of stress. It also means that you'll go to her party, you'll behave with complete propriety, and you'll make very sure that it's a complete success. Do you understand that, Philippa?'

She gulped very hard. 'Yes,' she somehow managed to get out. What else could she say, pinned down by those implacable blue eyes?

James kept her locked in her chair for a few more seconds with just the force of his gaze. Then he turned round and left the room, and Philippa slumped down with relief.

The relief didn't last, though. All those personal revelations about James were still whirling round inside her head. And now she had an engagement party to face!

In fact, the entire evening had been very sobering. That admission from James about the way his brother had died... Philippa gave a small, involuntary shiver because she could imagine only too vividly how it must feel to hold yourself responsible for the death of someone so close to you.

And there had been the second revelation, about his proposed marriage. That made her shiver all over again, but in a very different way. What had his bride-to-be been like? Philippa found that she just couldn't stop wondering. Tall? Slim? Beautiful? Aristocratic?

Probably all of those things, she told herself with a quick flare of jealousy that she couldn't suppress. But selfish, too. A woman who had wanted the title, the wealth, the status that marriage to James would bring, but not the responsibility of two children who had so recently lost their parents, children who would demand a lot of love and attention.

Philippa sighed. She would have adored a challenge like that, and the chance of a ready-made family.

And James Haverford as her husband?

That thought popped into her head out of nowhere, startling her so much that she nearly fell off her chair.

No, she told herself with rising alarm. *No*!

But it was amazing how hard it was to get rid of that thought, once it had lodged itself inside her mind.

Philippa slept badly that night, and knew that James was entirely responsible for her insomnia.

When she finally got up, a long shower refreshed her and got rid of the faint, tense ache behind her eyes. Neither James nor Stephanie turned up for breakfast, so she ate her meal in peace and then went in search of Richardson.

She found him washing down one of the cars outside the row of garages, converted from old stables, at the back of the house.

'Here, let me help,' she said, taking the hose from him. 'You wash and I'll rinse.'

He looked doubtful. 'I don't know. You're a guest here——'

'Oh, don't be so stuffy,' she said with a grin. 'I'm not a visiting duchess or countess. And even if I were it wouldn't make any difference. You wouldn't have to bow and scrape to me.'

Richardson smiled back at her. 'You sound like His Lordship. He doesn't like any ceremony. Doesn't even like to be called His Lordship, but everyone still does it, of course. They've been doing it for generations around here, and old habits die hard. His mother is quite different, of course; Lady Haverford likes everything very formal. No one would ever dare think of addressing her by her Christian name.'

His mention of James's mother reminded Philippa why she was here.

'Lady Haverford is organising a party this Saturday to introduce me to everyone,' she said with a small grimace. 'What on earth do I wear? James says that it's going to be an informal party, but I'm not sure what they mean by informal around here. If a friend of mine gave an informal party, I'd go along in jeans and a T-shirt. I don't think Lady Haverford would approve of that, though!'

'You're right,' agreed Richardson. 'Informal simply means that evening gowns and dinner-jackets aren't compulsory. Many of the guests will probably wear them, though. They know that Lady Haverford likes everyone to be dressed correctly. You may even see the odd tiara—a couple of Her Ladyship's friends are dowager duchesses, and they love dressing the part.'

'I haven't *got* an evening gown,' Philippa said with a worried frown. 'And I certainly haven't got a tiara!'

'Then wear something dark and simple,' Richardson advised. 'A plain black dress would be very suitable. And a string of pearls, if you've got them.'

'No, I haven't,' she said resignedly. 'I don't even like pearls.' She sighed. 'This party is going to be a disaster, isn't it?'

'Of course not,' he said reassuringly. 'Look, don't worry. I'm going to be on duty Saturday night, so I'll probably be around for most of the evening, serving drinks. If you need advice about anything, just come over and ask.'

'I'm bound to knock something over. Or spill my drink,' she predicted glumly. 'I always get clumsy when I'm nervous.'

'You'll be fine,' Richardson said at once. 'And there's absolutely nothing to be nervous about. It'll be just a lot of rather dull people standing around drinking, eating and talking. All you've got to do is charm the men, smile sweetly at the women, and laugh politely when someone makes a joke.'

'Are you trying to warn me that the evening's going to be very boring?'

'Let's just say that Her Ladyship's parties aren't quite as infamous as His Lordship's.'

Philippa's eyes shot wide open. 'James holds parties here?'

Richardson suddenly grinned. 'Only when Miss Stephanie is away at school and Master Jonathan is staying in London. His Lordship's parties are very grown-up affairs!'

Philippa was instantly intrigued. '*How* grown-up?'

'The guest lists would make any gossip columnist kill for an invitation.' He glanced round, as if to make sure no one else was listening. 'I've seen some of the most beautiful women in the world walk through that front entrance,' he said confidentially. 'And I've heard that some of them fought for an invitation! A lot of them were famous faces, too—you'd recognise them instantly. And one or two of them have come back again, only on their own. For a weekend that's a lot quieter and more private, if you understand what I mean.'

Philippa understood very well! And found herself transfixed by the jealousy that streaked through her.

Don't feel like that, *don't*, she told herself vehemently. It's none of your business whom James invites here. Or for what purpose!

But she couldn't stop thinking about it. Or feeling consumed by jealousy.

'Well, thanks for all your help,' she said to Richardson in what she hoped was a normal voice. 'I've—I've got to go now. I've got things to do.'

She escaped quickly and rushed up to her room, where she sat down on the edge of the great four-poster bed until she had that awful surge of jealousy under control.

This has got to stop, she told herself, biting her lip very hard. You can't behave like this just because James has invited beautiful women here for the weekend!

Only that made her think of James walking beside those women up the dark oak treads on the spiral staircase—along the upstairs gallery—his hand sliding round their waists—going into his room—— Her skin went ice-cold and she began to shake slightly. She had never felt real jealousy before, but she was certainly experiencing it now. And she didn't like it!

You should be thinking about Jonathan, she reminded herself a little frantically. *Jonathan.*

But the shameful truth was that it wasn't Jonathan who dominated all her waking thoughts, and even appeared in her dreams. It was James.

It doesn't mean anything, Philippa tried to convince herself. You're just fascinated by him. He's unlike anyone you've ever met—or are likely to meet! And he's so experienced. He knows exactly how to hook a woman—and keep her hooked!

She decided that it was time she made a very firm resolution. No more thinking about James—only Jonathan. And she would begin by concentrating on this engagement party and making a good impression on everyone there—even Lady Haverford!

Philippa spent the next hour rummaging through the clothes she had brought with her, trying to find something suitable to wear for a party given by a dowager countess. She finally decided that she didn't have any choice. Richardson was right—the most suitable thing would be a little black dress. Luckily, she had brought one with her, a short, stretchy, go-anywhere and do-anything dress, so plain that no one could possibly object to it. With her hair swept up into a tidy knot on top of her head, she should look quite acceptable.

When the evening of the party finally arrived, she showered and then spent ages trying to get her make-up right, subtle and not too obvious. Then she began to struggle with her hair, sweeping the long, glossy strands up and twisting them into place. Because she was nervous, she was all fingers and thumbs, and kept dropping pins everywhere. She finally managed to secure it into a knot, and gave a sigh of relief.

'Now for the dress,' she murmured to herself. She wriggled into it, smoothed it into place, and then anxiously looked at her reflection.

A very subdued Philippa stared back at her. The dark dress seemed to drain the colour from her face, the severe hairstyle didn't suit her, and the matching black shoes she had put on were pinching her toes.

A rebellious light began to flash in her eyes. 'Why *should* I dress like a frump, just to please the Haverfords?' she demanded of herself out loud. She was suddenly annoyed by the way she was beginning to give in submissively to the demands they made on her. 'Before I came here, I was independent and ran my own life. And I wore clothes that I liked and felt comfortable in. I think that it's time I went back to being the real me!'

She pulled off the dress and threw it over a nearby chair, kicked off the shoes, and shook her hair loose until it cascaded down over her shoulders. Then she reached into the wardrobe and took out a dress that she had earlier discarded as completely unsuitable.

It had been a very generous present from one of her best friends, who was a model. It was an outrageous shade of pink, with a tight and slinky bodice and a skirt overlaid with layers of fringes which swung seductively around her hips as she moved. Philippa had treated herself to a pair of matching vivid pink sandals, thin-strapped and high-heeled, which made her legs look incredibly long, and she put them on. She didn't bother with jewellery—the dress made enough of a statement! Then she marched out of the room before she completely lost her nerve.

The party was going to be held in the Great Hall. During the day, Philippa had seen the staff efficiently bustling in and out under the watchful eye of Braddock, the butler. They had obviously been through this routine dozens of times before, and knew exactly what needed to be done. There had been no sign of Lady Haverford herself—for which Philippa had been very grateful!—but she knew that the Dowager Countess would have arrived by now and be in the hall, ready to meet her guests.

From the window of the upstairs gallery, Philippa could see the sleek, shiny cars pulling up outside the Manor. Don't be nervous, she instructed herself sternly. There's absolutely no difference between these people and you—except that they've got titles and pots of money!

She held her head up high, straightened her shoulders, and went down the stairs with a great outward show of confidence. *No one* was going to know that her heart was hammering away at breakneck speed.

The doors to the Great Hall stood wide open and she stood in the entrance for a couple of moments, trying to work up enough courage to walk inside. Candles burned in the great gothic chandelier suspended from the high, beamed ceiling, and there were more banks of candles in ornate wrought-iron stands set around the hall. Philippa thought that was rather over the top because the evening sun was still shining outside, but she had to admit that it was very effective. The atmosphere was warm and intimate, and the old, dark panelling gleamed richly in the golden light.

Braddock, the butler, was standing just inside the doorway, and as he turned his head and saw her he gave her a very frosty look. Philippa had seen little of him during her stay here, but she knew instinctively that he didn't approve of her. He looked a very stiff and stuffy man, and he no doubt thought that she had no business even setting foot inside a place like Sherringborne Manor.

'Miss Philippa Martin,' he announced, his tone as disapproving as his face.

Every pair of eyes in the hall immediately swivelled around to fix on her.

You are *not* going to turn round and bolt, Philippa told herself firmly. She made herself stand very still and hoped that she looked cool and composed. That wasn't easy when she was the centre of such intense curiosity!

She saw that Lady Haverford's guests were mostly middle-aged or older, and nearly all of them were very formally dressed. The men wore black dinner-jackets and bow-ties, and the women's dresses were mainly in dark or muted colours. And there were pearls everywhere! Philippa noted wryly. Richardson had been right—she should have worn her black dress and borrowed some pearls if she wanted to fit in.

In her short, vivid dress with its frivolous fringes, she stuck out like a sore thumb. Although the men certainly seemed to like it! Several of them were already beginning to look at her with some interest.

Then Lady Haverford detached herself from a small group of guests, and Philippa swallowed hard and wished that she hadn't given in to that crazy impulse to change her clothes. The Dowager Countess wore a dark navy dress in heavy satin, with diamonds sparkling discreetly in her ears.

She approached Philippa, and as she drew near her gaze fixed on the dazzling pink dress. Then she gave a small but visible shudder. 'My dear,' she murmured in a low voice, 'we really must shop for some suitable clothes for you next week.'

'I'm very happy with my wardrobe,' Philippa said defensively.

'I'm sure it's very suitable for your present lifestyle,' Lady Haverford said pointedly. 'But your life will change when you marry Jonathan, and you obviously need a little guidance. That dress, for example—not *quite* right for the occasion.'

Philippa bit back the retort she was longing to make. She remembered James's instructions—nothing was to be allowed to upset his mother. She could just imagine his reaction if she began the evening with a stand-up row with Lady Haverford!

'Whatever happens in the future, I don't intend to let it change anything about me,' she said, carefully keeping her tone firm but very polite. 'Including my clothes.'

Lady Haverford raised one eyebrow, as if surprised that Philippa had had the nerve to answer back. 'We'll discuss it later,' was all she said, though. 'Come and meet some of my guests.'

Philippa found herself being very efficiently escorted around the hall, and introduced to different groups of people. The men seemed to like her and warm to her very quickly, even those who had looked rather starchy on first introduction. Many of the women exchanged swift, sympathetic glances with Lady Haverford, however. Those looks clearly said everything. Yes, Philippa was pretty, but really not at all *suitable*.

Philippa gritted her teeth, though, and kept smiling politely. Then she felt the fine hairs on the nape of her neck stand right up on end, and she knew at once who had just walked into the room. She refused to turn round and look at James, however, and instead began to talk animatedly to the small group of people Lady Haverford had left her with. They had been asking about her career, and seemed intrigued by her reply.

'A dancer?' repeated a rather overdressed woman. 'The ballet, I suppose?'

'No,' said Philippa, with a wry look at her long legs. 'I grew too tall. I dance in summer shows, cabaret, pantomime, anywhere I can get a job.' She could see eyebrows beginning to rise, and knew that she was providing the women with a whole new source of gossip. Jonathan Haverford had got involved with a showgirl!

'Where are you working now?' asked another of the women.

'I'm out of work at the moment,' she admitted. 'Although I've just come back from a couple of weeks in Tunisia.' Her eyes began to gleam as she realised she could make their raised eyebrows almost disappear into their hairlines. 'I had a temporary job as a——'

'As part of a small entertainment group,' James cut in smoothly.

The sound of his voice made every one of her nerves jump. She hadn't realised that he had silently moved over to stand behind her. His blue eyes locked on to hers and conveyed a silent message. It would be *most* unwise to mention the word 'belly-dancer'.

Philippa didn't quite have the nerve to ignore that message. Then she caught her breath as James lightly slid his hand under her arm. She tried to draw away, but found that his light grip was deceptive. She couldn't actually move without getting involved in an awkward and embarrassing struggle.

'I'm afraid I have to take Philippa away from you for a while,' James said politely. 'There are other people she has to meet.'

His fingers locked a little more tightly around her and he steered her over to the far side of the hall. He didn't introduce her to any more guests, though. In fact, he led her to a shadowed area beneath the minstrel's gallery, well away from the other guests.

'What are you doing?' she asked fiercely. 'And why did you interrupt me when I was talking to those people? I wasn't ashamed to tell them that I was a belly-dancer for a few weeks!'

'This is my mother's party,' he reminded her grimly. 'And I don't intend to let you do or say anything to embarrass her in front of her friends.'

'And she's going to be embarrassed if I tell everyone I was a belly-dancer?'

'Of course,' he said cuttingly. 'And you know it.'

She was silent because he was right, of course.

'I warned you what would happen if you tried anything like this,' he reminded her, his eyes locking on to hers.

'I know,' she said defiantly. 'But I was angry because your mother was rude about my dress. All right, I *know* it isn't right for a party like this,' Philippa admitted, beginning to feel slightly ashamed of her behaviour, 'but I didn't want to wear something dull and frumpy.'

'I can't imagine you ever looking frumpy,' James said in an unexpectedly dry tone.

It was almost a compliment, and certainly not the reply she had expected. At the same time she realised that he was still holding on to her arm—and he didn't seem to have any intention of letting go!

Philippa's skin already felt uncomfortably hot where his fingers were locked against it, and there was something in his expression that was beginning to disturb her—a darkness in his eyes that made her stomach suddenly flutter. And he looked so very impressive tonight in his dark dinner-jacket, with the crisp and immaculate shirt so white against his supple, lightly tanned skin.

'Don't you think that you should—er—let go of me?' she suggested nervously. 'People are beginning to stare.'

James looked down at his hand, as if he had almost forgotten that it was gripping her arm. Very slowly, he relaxed his fingers, but it was several more moments before he finally released her. Then he abruptly turned away from her and walked off to join another group of guests.

Philippa knew that she should feel more relaxed now that he had moved away, but she didn't. There had been the strangest expression on his face, and a fierce, almost uncontrolled look in his eyes.

She helped herself to a glass of champagne and gulped it down very quickly, hoping that it would help to steady her nerves. It didn't, though. Nor did the second glass.

She began chattering too brightly to some of the guests, trying to ignore James's presence. But that was impossible. Even when she couldn't see him she could feel his brilliant blue gaze boring into her back. And when they came suddenly face to face again as they circulated among the guests, they simply stared at each other for a few intensely charged seconds before forcing themselves to move on.

Philippa found it increasingly impossible to concentrate on what she was saying or doing, and she just hoped she wasn't talking complete gibberish! And what about the other guests? Had they noticed what was going on?

Philippa certainly hoped not, because they were Lady Haverford's friends and they would be sure to tell her.

Towards the end of the evening, she found herself standing alone for a couple of minutes. She gave a small sigh of relief because the ordeal was almost over; the party was slowly winding down. In another hour the guests would all be gone, and she could escape to the safety of her room. Only, was anywhere in this house safe, when every inch of it belonged to James?

Then every muscle in her body locked with sudden tension as she heard his voice in her ear.

'Come with me,' he ordered softly.

She hadn't heard him approach silently from behind, and the sound of his voice did quite extraordinary things to her nervous system.

'Where to?' she asked, her heart abruptly thumping so hard that she found it hard to breathe.

But he didn't answer her. Instead his eyes burned into hers for a few seconds. Then he swung round and left the hall.

Philippa told herself that she shouldn't go with him, she absolutely *shouldn't*. But her legs were already carrying her after him.

The brilliance of the Great Hall was soon left behind, and James was just a dark shadow in front of her as he led her on along dimly lit corridors, finally opening a door and going into a room that was in complete darkness.

Philippa *knew* that this was the time to stop, turn round, run back to the safety of the Great Hall, bring some sanity back into her life. Instead she followed him inside.

James switched on a small lamp, which gave off just enough light to let her see that she was in his private drawing-room. Then he turned round to face her.

'Come closer,' he ordered, and there was a harsh edge to his voice, as if he didn't want to do this, but simply couldn't stop himself.

Again she obeyed, which was crazy, especially since she could now see the light that burned in those fierce blue eyes.

His hand came up and twisted a long strand of her hair around his fingers.

'What—what are you doing?' she said unsteadily.

'You know very well,' he growled at her. 'What I've wanted to do all evening. And what you've wanted as well.'

'I haven't, I really haven't,' she lied a little desperately. It was too late, though, and of course she had known it all along. Whatever was happening between them—and she was beginning to realise now what it was, but that just made her even more scared—it was starting to gallop headlong out of control.

James's fingers delved deep into the rest of her hair, pulled on its silky thickness, bringing her face nearer to his. Then he kissed her, his mouth hot and hard, and the intensity of the kiss stunned her. This wasn't some casual flirtation, it was——

Philippa clamped down hard on the end of that thought. It was too terrifying.

His kisses swiftly turned her emotions inside out, and after a couple of minutes she couldn't think at all. She found that she was straining to get even closer to him, and his hands instantly helped. They locked around her, pulling her so tightly against him that the hard outline of his body was imprinted against hers, from the strong muscles in his arms to the broad width of his chest, the flatness of his stomach, the rigid stance of his legs, and the powerful surge of desire between them.

That blatant announcement of his desire made her shake a little. Then a flush of colour swept over her face as she realised that she wanted to *touch* him; it was hard to hold back her hands; she had to remind herself frantically that she couldn't, mustn't, this really was wrong, all wrong! But he was already stroking *her*, the seductive fringes of the vivid pink dress brushing softly against his fingers as they slid easily under the clinging material, then down and down, bringing an instant wave of pleasure that hit her with a force that almost made her legs buckle.

And if he could touch her like that, then it must be all right to touch him, and for just a few moments Philippa allowed herself the forbidden pleasure; the hardness of his body beat against the palm of her hand, and the world stood still.

'You know exactly how to do this, don't you?' James muttered angrily in her ear. 'How many times have you played this game?'

His words shocked her into withdrawal. She wanted to blurt out that this wasn't a game for her, it was a devastating experience that she didn't even know how to handle, but he wasn't interested in listening to any explanation. Anger was overridden by desire again as his hand found her breast with a skill and single-minded purpose that warned her that nothing would easily stop him tonight. He caressed her through the soft material, then impatiently pulled down the stretchy top of her dress and seized hold of her warm, exposed skin. His fingertips explored roughly but not painfully, except that the pleasure itself was so intense that it almost hurt, and it left her hungry for more, more.

James was very willing to supply it. He played with her nipple until Philippa heard the sound of her own voice moaning out loud. He stroked the soft, swollen flesh, teased and tickled. Then his mouth joined in the assault; he bent his dark head and let his tongue trail pleasure across her burning skin, and he kissed and lightly sucked until her entire body threatened to melt under the onslaught.

Then James pulled her dress back into place, and she heard her voice again, this time begging him not to stop.

'Don't worry,' he said roughly. 'I don't intend to stop. You've made very sure of that, haven't you?'

But she hadn't done anything except respond blindly to his overwhelming assault on all her senses. His fingers were already threading their way through her hair again; he couldn't seem to resist the silken touch of it drifting through his hands. Philippa stood very still, scarcely breathing; she adored the gentle tugging on her hair as his fingers ran through it in soft, sensual movements. She adored *him*, she realised numbly. And she wanted to be kissed again!

James made her wait and wait, though; long, painful minutes slowly passed before his mouth returned to hers, and this time with a deliberate and tantalising lightness, his lips barely touching hers at first. She ached for more and he knew it; his tongue began to lick softly until her lips were moist and tasted of him. And his hands had left her hair now; instead they played with the fringed skirt of her dress, sometimes sliding over it, sometimes slipping underneath it, subtly leading her on and on until she hardly knew where she was or what she was doing.

Philippa's own hands tentatively began to move, feeling the heat of his skin through the fine material of his shirt and the fast, heavy beat of his heart. The hammering increased as her fingers traced the outline of his powerful ribcage, his hard, masculine nipples, the beginning of the flat, tense muscles of his stomach.

She didn't need to be told that he wanted her to go further, that he ached to feel her gentle, intimate touch again, even though the frustrated pleasure would be almost a pain. And she could feel the intense anger that still surged beneath the desire; anger that he couldn't control this. She felt him silently fight to keep his mouth away from hers, but then he gave in with a dark growl and a swift, intense kiss urged her on, and the shadowed silence of the room was broken only by James's quick, heavy breathing as he pulled her close, so close that she could hear her heart beating in the same rhythm as his own. Another kiss followed, fiercely intense, dark and bruising, bringing its own unique brand of pleasure.

Caught up in the fresh flood of confused and turbulent emotions, neither of them heard the muted click of heels in the corridor outside, or even noticed when the door opened. The voice that cut through the sensual atmosphere that filled the room made both of them instantly spring apart, though.

'James, our guests are beginning to leave and I can't find Philippa. She should be there to say goodnight——' Lady Haverford began briskly. Then she abruptly stopped speaking, and Philippa, released at last from that final, heart-stopping kiss, slowly turned to face the icy blue gaze of the Dowager Countess of Sherringborne.

CHAPTER SEVEN

ALL trace of desire instantly vanished and a terrible silence hung over the room. James met his mother's eyes levelly, but said nothing. Philippa simply wanted to sink through the floor and completely disappear. She felt so embarrassed, so guilty, so *ashamed*.

In the end, she couldn't stand the awful silence any longer.

'I'm sorry,' she blurted out. She knew that it was a stupid, totally inadequate thing to say, but it was all she could manage.

Lady Haverford looked at her so coldly that Philippa half expected to turn into a column of ice.

'I might not have considered you a suitable match for my grandson, but I thought you would at least know how to behave while you were a guest in this house,' she said in a frozen tone.

'The fault was mine,' James said in a very controlled voice.

Lady Haverford's eyebrows rose expressively. 'Really? I didn't notice Philippa struggling to get away.'

'It was just something that happened,' Philippa said a little desperately. 'We never meant—*I* never meant——'

'I'm not interested in excuses,' Lady Haverford cut in. She was leaning heavily on her stick now, and looked very white, as if the full implication of the scene she had just walked in on was finally beginning to sink in.

James turned to her. 'Philippa, go upstairs. I'll deal with this.'

'But I was involved,' she reminded him shakily. 'I think that I ought to stay here.'

'Go to your room,' James repeated grimly.

Philippa didn't need telling a third time. Her nerve had completely cracked by now, and she ran out of the room so quickly that she only caught one last quick glimpse of James's face, fierce and dark, as she dashed past him.

She rushed straight up the stairs and into her bedroom, where she threw herself on to the bed and curled up into a small ball. Of all the things that could have happened, that had to be the very worst! It was bad enough that she hadn't been able to resist following James into that room, that she had hungered so much after his kisses, guiltily enjoyed every single thing he had done to her. But to be caught in the middle of it by Lady Haverford! And on the night of the party to celebrate Philippa's engagement to Jonathan.

Philippa gave a small groan. She should never have let that party take place. She should have admitted that things had changed—*she* had changed—and that she just couldn't go through with her engagement any longer. Too late now, though; the dreadful damage was done.

You're the one who's caused all this trouble, she told herself miserably. You made the wrong decisions, the wrong choices, and now everyone's suffering because of it.

She felt an irrational desire to punish herself. But she didn't know how, except perhaps by finally telling the truth. But what good would that really do? She could just imagine their faces as she announced that she had fallen in love with the wrong Haverford!

Her throat went very dry. She had finally admitted it! It wasn't just an irresistible physical attraction she felt towards James. It was more—a whole lot more! She shook her head in fresh confusion. What was she going to do *now*? She didn't know. Oh, this had to be the biggest mess of her entire life!

Exhausted by the events of the evening, Philippa eventually fell asleep still fully dressed and curled up in the centre of the bed. In the morning, she woke up to find that she was wearing the bright pink fringed dress, and sleepily tried to remember why. Then *everything* that had happened last night suddenly rushed back into her head, and she immediately sat bolt upright.

How on earth was she going to face the day ahead? she wondered with a small gulp. Lady Haverford would almost certainly demand an explanation. What could she possibly say? How could all the apologies in the world make up for that terrible moment when Lady Haverford had walked in and found her and James together?

And, of course, there was James himself to face!

Philippa fervently wished that she could hide away in the safety of her room all day. It would only be putting off her dreaded encounter with the Haverford family, though. Far better to get it over with straight away.

She showered and dressed, and then crept downstairs on legs that were distinctly wobbly. She stood hesitantly in the corridor for a long time before eventually making her way to the breakfast-room. The door stood ajar and she nervously pushed it fully open, then sagged with relief when she saw that the room was empty.

Plates of food were set out on the side-table, but she didn't even touch them. She knew that she wouldn't be able to eat. She poured herself some coffee, then sat down at the table, her fingers twisting together edgily.

When she heard the door open, her heart felt as if it had just turned right over, and she didn't dare look round. A few moments later, though, James slid into the seat opposite her.

She finally found the nerve to raise her gaze to his. In the bright morning light, every feature of his face showed with absolute clarity, from the brilliant blue of his eyes to the hard, sensual line of his mouth, the dark, arrogant slant of his eyebrows to the faint shadows of sleeplessness, the only indication of the after-effects of last night's traumatic events.

'I thought you might have run away after that unfortunate scene with my mother,' James said at last in a hard voice.

'Unfortunate?' she echoed in disbelief. 'That's something of an understatement! And I don't run away from my problems,' she added with a touch of defiance.

'I'm glad that you're ready to admit that we do have a problem.'

'It would be hard *not* to admit that,' she retorted. At the same time, though, she could hardly drag her eyes away from his mouth. His beautiful, hard, kissable mouth.

She almost groaned out loud. How could she even be thinking about such a thing right now? Every day she seemed to be sliding further into a great emotional swamp that was eventually going to suck her right under. What was she going to do next? she wondered with rising alarm. Blurt out that she *loved* him?

She felt her face growing hot, and her mouth and throat were completely dry. Oh, please don't let me do anything as stupid as that! she prayed silently.

James leant forward, his eyes fixed on her face, as if he was intent on seeing right inside her head. Suddenly terrified that he would be able to read her thoughts, she reached blindly for her cup of coffee. Her nerveless fingers immediately knocked it over and she jumped to her feet. She grabbed a napkin, but at the same time sent a plate flying on to the floor, where it smashed.

A moment later, she found her hands caught in James's cool grip.

'There's no need to go to pieces,' he said drily. 'My mother has returned home; you won't have to face her today. And if *I'm* the one making you nervous, just relax. I'll keep my distance this morning. Unless you decide that you don't want me to,' he added in a rather different tone of voice.

'You're already touching me,' Philippa said a little frantically.

He immediately released her hands. 'Better?'

No, it wasn't. The trouble was, of course, that she *wanted* to be touched. She really ached for his touch all the time. Telling him that would be absolutely insane, though. It would mean that all the advantages would be on his side, and she would have absolutely no defences left against him.

And she really needed some kind of defence. She had realised by now that she simply couldn't handle James Haverford. He was completely beyond her experience, in every way.

James efficiently picked up the broken pieces of plate and mopped up the spilt coffee, while Philippa slowly sat down again.

'What—what did your mother say last night, after I left?' she asked apprehensively.

He gave a rather grim smile. 'I don't think that you want to know.'

He was right. She didn't. But she couldn't just forget about it. She thought that she was going to remember that look on Lady Haverford's face for the rest of her life!

'When she walked in like that—it was awful,' she said with a small shudder.

'It was certainly bad timing,' James agreed.

'Bad timing!' she repeated incredulously. 'It wasn't the timing that was the problem. We shouldn't even have been there. And we certainly shouldn't have been doing—what we were doing,' she finished with a small shiver as she remembered exactly what *had* happened between them.

'There's little point in regretting something that's already happened,' he said in a controlled voice. 'And there's a very simple solution, something that will stop the inevitable gossip and take some of the pressure off everyone.'

'What?' she asked warily.

'First, I think you'd better read this.' He reached into his pocket and brought out a letter. 'It arrived for you this morning. As usual, Jonathan's shown his usual excellent sense of timing.'

'Jonathan?' Philippa said, biting her lip with a fresh rush of apprehension. 'This is a letter from Jonathan?'

She took it from him very gingerly, as if it were red-hot. She knew that she didn't want to read it, not this morning, when she was still so full of guilt over her own behaviour.

'I think that I'd like to read it in private,' she said carefully.

'There's no need for that,' James told her shortly. 'I already know what's in it.'

'You've *read* it?' she said accusingly. 'You opened my private letter?'

'Of course not. But I also had a letter from Jonathan this morning. I know what he's written to tell you.'

Philippa looked at him very guardedly. Something was going on here, something that was beginning to make her feel extremely uneasy.

Slowly, she opened the envelope. It was very hard to keep her hands steady with James standing so close. His forceful presence made her think about last night and she knew that she shouldn't; she had to concentrate on her letter.

She slid the pages out of the envelope, and the first few hurriedly scrawled lines told her everything that she needed to know.

My dear Philippa,

By the time you've finished reading this, you're probably going to hate me. I don't want to hurt you because you know how fond I am of you, but I think it's best if I just come right out and tell you the truth. I've met a girl here, on a climbing expedition, and I've—well, I've just fallen for her completely. This is the real thing, and you're probably never going to forgive me—I know that I don't *deserve* to be forgiven—and I'm sorry, sorry, sorry, but I realise now that I simply can't marry you...

The letter went on for a couple more pages. More apologies, more about the girl—her name was Nicky—and their plans to travel on from Nepal to the Far East, and then to Australia. Then one final long apology before Jonathan had scribbled his name.

Philippa was absolutely stunned. She had been so full of guilt, and frantically trying to think of a way of gently telling him that she wanted to end their unofficial engagement, but *he* had been the one who had actually ended the relationship!

James's eyes were fixed intently on her face, as if trying to gauge her reaction. 'I did try to warn you,' he said a little harshly. 'Jonathan falls in—and out—of love very easily.'

'He must have met her just days after he left England,' she said dazedly. 'Why didn't he tell me sooner? I needn't have come here to Sherringborne. Needn't have——'

'Needn't have met me?' James finished for her in a taut voice as she bit back those last few words.

Philippa remained silent because that was exactly what she had been about to blurt out.

'Jonathan wrote a similar letter to me, explaining the situation.' James paused for a moment, then added, 'He also asked me if I'd look after you.'

'Oh, I think that you've already done that, don't you?' she said in a brittle voice. Then she suddenly rounded on him. 'This doesn't make everything all right,' she said explosively. 'Last night we didn't *know* that Jonathan had sent this letter, but we still—we still——'

'We still managed to shock my mother. And provide the staff with enough gossip to last for the rest of the year,' James said darkly. 'I don't need to be reminded how badly we both behaved. And we have a duty to put that right.'

'And how do you suggest we do that?' Philippa demanded.

'There's a very simple way to stop all the rumours, and make sure that my mother isn't completely humiliated. Instead of marrying Jonathan, you'll marry *me*,' James ordered.

* * *

Philippa began to be quite sure that she was hallucinating. James couldn't possibly have said that!

'M-marry you?' she stuttered in a voice so unlike her own that she didn't even recognise it.

'It's the obvious solution.'

She began to recover just a fraction. 'It isn't at all obvious to me! Last night there was a party here to celebrate my engagement to *Jonathan*,' she reminded him.

'It was an unofficial party for close family friends and relatives. They'll be discreetly told of the change of plan. Later on there'll be an official announcement and party.'

'And you think that everyone will just accept that?' she said incredulously.

'I'll make very sure that they accept it,' he assured her in a grim tone.

Her legs suddenly began to shake so badly that she had to sit down. Marriage to James Haverford! She could have everything that she longed for—if she was crazy enough to accept his proposal!

'No,' she said, shaking her head dazedly. 'I can't do it.'

James gripped her arms and hauled her back to her feet, so that she was forced to face him head-on. 'I didn't say that you were being given a choice. This is the obvious way to resolve the situation, and I intend that we should take it.'

'Well, it doesn't seem at all obvious to me,' she retorted with fresh determination. 'Or even necessary! All we have to do is announce that I'm not going to marry Jonathan. The Haverford family isn't going to be involved in any gossip or scandal. Only your mother knows about—about last night,' she said, her tongue tripping slightly over her words.

'Wrong,' James said tersely, his hands still locked around her arms, not allowing her to move an inch away from him. 'One of the staff apparently overheard something through the half-open door, and rumours and stories are flying all over Sherringborne this morning.'

Philippa went bright red. 'You mean——?'

'Almost everyone on the estate will soon know—or try to guess—what happened between us. The pressure on my mother will be intolerable; she loathes scandal of any kind. I won't put her health at risk by subjecting her to that. A quick announcement today of our forthcoming marriage will put a swift end to the rumours, and stop any further speculation.'

'And what about *me*?' she demanded. 'What *I* want?'

His face altered, his mouth became harder, and a cynical light shone in his eyes. 'Oh, I know what you want, Philippa,' he said softly. 'What you've wanted all along. The money, the status, one of the most magnificent houses in the country. And you can have it. It's the price I'm willing to pay for my mother's health and peace of mind, and to prevent any scandal being attached to the Haverford name.'

Her shoulders suddenly slumped. He still believed that she only wanted him because of who he was, what he owned. And she was sure that all the words in the world couldn't convince him otherwise.

'Then you're saying that this will be a marriage of convenience,' she said in a choked voice. 'Not a real marriage at all.'

His hand ran lightly up her arm, leaving an army of intensely pleasurable goose-bumps in its wake.

'Oh, no,' he said, a purely sensual note suddenly entering his voice and sending fresh shivers right through her. 'On our marriage night I shall most certainly expect you in my bed. We both know that this isn't a great love match, but we certainly want each other. Why deny ourselves what little pleasure this marriage will bring?'

Philippa shivered involuntarily at the thought of sharing his bed—and his life. All she had to do was say yes.

And she wanted to. She *ached* to say that one word. The emotions that were running pell-mell through her were nothing like the friendly feelings that she had had for Jonathan. These were fierce and deep, frighteningly uncontrollable.

James gave a sudden, dark smile of satisfaction, as if yet again he knew exactly how his offer of marriage had confused—and excited—her.

His fingers slid possessively over her breast, and his smile deepened as he felt her tremble. 'I like knowing that I can make you react like that,' he murmured. 'I like knowing that I'm the only one who can do it.'

'Do you think that's something to be proud of?' she said in a slightly choked voice.

'Yes,' he said at once. 'So many people can't make each other feel anything at all.' His palm rubbed lightly against the small, hard nipple pressing against him, and then his hand moved down to her waist and rested there, feeling the small movements of her hot and aching body. 'You want more, don't you?' he challenged her softly. 'And you can have it. Just say yes to my proposal.'

'I don't see that marriage would solve our problems,' Philippa managed to get out, fighting the almost irresistible urge to agree to absolutely anything he asked her.

'It would immediately kill the local gossip and any interest from the Press. No one's interested in a relationship once it's been made legal. It's only illicit affairs that are newsworthy and provide the fuel for scandal.'

'I think you're exaggerating,' she forced herself to say. 'No one's really going to blow this up into a full-scale scandal.'

'Don't be so naïve,' James said more harshly. 'There are reporters from the gutter Press who would kill to get their hands on a story like this. And you're intelligent enough to know the fun they would have inventing the headlines. "The Earl and the Belly-dancer",' he quoted in dark disgust. '"Love Triangle at Stately Home". And that would only be the beginning. Once a story like that catches on, it can run and run. And what they don't know, or can't find out, they'll invent.'

Philippa gave a huge shiver. 'You're exaggerating,' she repeated, although without any real conviction.

'Am I?' he said grimly. 'Try it and see!' Then his mouth set into a dangerous line. 'Or perhaps you *want* to try it?' he suggested, his eyes turning ice blue. 'Perhaps you're looking forward to a whole new career as an overnight celebrity. The talk shows, the Press interviews, the kiss-and-tell revelations, the front-page photographs——'

'No!' she said vehemently. 'No, that's *not* what I want.'

'It had better not be,' James warned, every inch of his body suddenly so threatening that, for the very first time, she felt slightly afraid of him.

'It isn't!' Philippa insisted.

'Then you agree to my solution to the problem?'

Before she could say anything, the door opened and Stephanie walked in. She looked at them standing so very close, James tense and dominating, Philippa very pale, and her eyes brightened with sudden interest.

'Hello, Uncle James,' she said demurely. Then her gaze rested on Philippa almost gleefully. 'Hello, Miss Martin. I didn't think you'd still be here this morning.'

James drew back from Philippa and looked at his niece. 'What are you talking about, Stephanie?'

'Well—there was some trouble last night, wasn't there?' Stephanie said delicately. 'I heard the staff talking about it in the kitchen. And when I went round to see Grandma, she was very angry about something. She wouldn't tell me what it was, though.'

'What did you overhear in the kitchen?' James asked tensely.

Stephanie gave a small shrug. 'Nothing very much. One of the part-time girls had sneaked off to an empty part of the house for a quick cigarette and saw something she shouldn't have—something very interesting—but they stopped talking about it when they saw me come in. I definitely heard Philippa's name, though.'

James's face darkened ominously and Philippa felt her legs begin to shake all over again.

'That's why I thought you might have packed up and run,' Stephanie went on, turning to face Philippa. 'Whatever happened, it was obviously your fault and Grandma is very upset and absolutely *furious*. And when Grandma gets angry, most people run for their lives!'

'Stephanie, that is enough!' James ordered, his authoritative tone immediately making his niece shut up and look rather subdued. She obviously didn't like it when her adored uncle spoke to her in that stern tone of voice.

Philippa's head was spinning even faster. So James was right—the household staff already knew all about last night. And soon the gossip would spread, everything would get blown up out of all proportion, and even Jonathan would be affected by it. This was terrible, the worst thing that had ever happened to her. And so much of it was her fault, because she just hadn't been able to fight her feelings for James. She couldn't fight them even now! And if she stayed, everything would just get worse.

'Stephanie's right,' she mumbled almost to herself. 'I've got to leave. Get as far away from here as possible.'

James's hand instantly locked on to her arm. 'You're not going anywhere,' he told her.

'Oh, let her go,' Stephanie said rudely. 'We'll all be better off without her.'

'Stephanie, you will apologise at once for that remark,' James said crisply.

For a moment Stephanie looked rebellious enough to disobey that order. Then she looked at her uncle's severe face and wisely changed her mind.

'I apologise,' she said, although she obviously hated saying those two words.

Philippa wished that James hadn't interfered. She knew that Stephanie was going to blame her for that stern rebuke from her uncle. Another black mark against her!

But James hadn't finished with his niece. 'Your attitude towards Philippa is going to have to change,' he told her. 'Her stay here isn't going to be short-term. You might as well know right now that I've ask her to marry me. And I intend that she should say yes.'

Stephanie instantly looked completely horrified. 'Marry her?' she repeated incredulously. 'But—you can't! Anyway, she's going to marry Jonathan.'

'That was a mistake,' James said in a very cool voice, as if he didn't like to be reminded in any way of Philippa's relationship with Jonathan. 'It was never an official engagement, and it's now over. My engagement to Philippa will certainly be official, though, and it will be announced in the very near future. I wanted you to know first.'

'What about Grandma?' demanded Stephanie. 'Have you told her?'

'No,' James said, his mouth tightening, as if he wasn't looking forward to that particular duty.

'She won't approve. Oh, you can't *do* this!' Stephanie said with a sudden rush of vehemence. She turned to Philippa. 'You've got to stop him. You can do it. All you've got to do is say you won't marry him!'

But Philippa was staring at James's mouth. That hard mouth that had entranced her from the very first moment she had seen it. And she was imagining what it would be like to feel it locked against hers in the darkness of the night. To hear his voice every single day. To share his life, be a part of it. Even, perhaps, to have his children...

'Yes, I am going to marry him,' she said in a voice that didn't sound in the least like her own.

CHAPTER EIGHT

PHILIPPA spent the next couple of days trying to convince herself that she had actually agreed to marry James. Every morning she woke up and told herself that it had been a completely mad thing to do, and she would put a stop to it this very day—in fact right now! But as soon as she came face to face with James, her mouth would dry up, her heart would start beating very fast, and she would be quite incapable of saying the actual words.

News of their intended marriage had already spread, and had obviously amazed absolutely everyone. She was aware of the staff staring at her curiously behind her back—and sometimes to her face! James was right about it putting an end to the more lurid gossip, though. Their engagement was news—astonishing news!—but not a scandal.

By the end of the week, however, Philippa was finding the strain a bit too much to take. She decided she had to escape from the house for a while, give herself a few hours away from the quizzical looks and whispering voices. She wandered out into the sunshine, but even the gardens didn't seem a refuge. She needed to get right away from Sherringborne for a few hours.

A couple of bicycles were kept in one of the old stables, and Philippa helped herself to one. She knew that there was a small market town a few miles away. She could easily cycle that far, and a change of scene might help her to get her scrambled thoughts and complicated emotions straightened out again.

The weather was still good, with a bright sun blazing down out of a clear blue sky as she cycled off down the drive. It was a long but fairly easy run to the market town, and she enjoyed the exercise; it was good to feel her muscles fully stretched. The town turned out to be surprisingly lively, with several interesting old buildings, and Philippa enjoyed just pottering around. She had a leisurely lunch and then browsed through the shops, buying a couple of personal items she needed.

It was late afternoon before she finally got back on the bike and began to cycle home to Sherringborne Manor.

Because she was in no hurry, and because there were so few cars that she didn't have to concentrate on the road ahead, she began to daydream as she pedalled. Silly daydreams, about James waiting for her at the Manor, missing her and pleased to see her. That was how she missed the private side-road that would have taken her directly back to the house.

She had cycled on for another mile before she finally realised her mistake. Philippa stopped and gave a rueful sigh. She really didn't feel like cycling all that way back again. Her legs were strong, but she had already cycled several miles today and she was definitely beginning to feel tired.

Then she noticed another side-road, about a hundred yards ahead, which seemed to head roughly in the direction of Sherringborne Manor. Was it worth taking a chance and hoping it would take her there? She knew that there was more than one approach road to the house.

She swung left and then pedalled on, grateful that the road was fairly level. She really was getting too tired to tackle any steep hills. Tall, elegant trees on either side shaded her from the heat of the late afternoon sun, and she soon settled into an easy rhythm that swiftly covered the ground.

She rounded a sharp corner, the trees disappeared, and she saw a house ahead. A very large and elegant house, set in a spacious, immaculate garden. On impulse, Philippa stopped. It made sense to knock and ask if she was going in the right direction for Sherringborne Manor. She didn't want to cycle on right through Dorset, getting more and more lost!

She left the bike at the gate and walked up the path that wound between formal flowerbeds. Then she knocked boldly on the front door.

No one came, and she began to think the house was empty. But, just as she was about to turn away, the door finally swung open. And then Philippa fervently wished that there *hadn't* been anyone at home, because she found herself facing Lady Haverford!

This imposing house was her 'cottage', Philippa realised with a gulp.

Lady Haverford's face was cold and distant. Philippa obviously wasn't a welcome visitor!

'I certainly never expected to see you here,' she said, her aristocratic features fixed in an expression of extreme hostility.

'I—I didn't know that *you* lived here,' Philippa stammered. 'I was lost; I just knocked to ask for directions. If I'd known this was your house, I wouldn't have—well, I'd have asked somewhere else...' Her voice trailed away in sheer nervousness. Then she was immediately annoyed with herself. Why was she so overawed by this one elderly woman? James's mother, she reminded herself. Her future mother-in-law! It really was quite ridiculous to be so frightened of her.

'My son tells me that he intends to marry you,' Lady Haverford said in an icily disapproving tone.

'Er—yes,' Philippa said. Then she added impulsively, 'Look, I know we got off to a bad start.' She remembered the night of the party, when Lady Haverford had walked in on her and James. 'A *very* bad start,' she admitted, her face reddening. 'But I'd like to try and explain how it happened. Then perhaps we can start afresh.'

Lady Haverford totally ignored Philippa's tentative offering of peace. Instead her blue gaze fixed on her without even a glimmer of warmth.

'You're totally unsuitable, of course,' she said in an autocratic tone. 'The marriage can't possibly work. Unfortunately, there's very little I can do to stop it. My son has always been very strong-willed. And completely single-minded when he decides that he wants something—or someone. It's a strange thing that his judgement—which is usually excellent—seems at fault where women are concerned. This is the second time he's made the wrong choice. His first fiancée didn't have the strength of character to take on joint responsibility with him for Jonathan and Stephanie. And now he intends to marry outside his own class, something which is always a mistake.'

Philippa forgot all about trying to be friendly—or even polite—to this woman.

'Now wait just a minute,' she said in growing outrage. 'Are you saying that I'm not good enough for James?'

'That's exactly what I'm saying,' Lady Haverford replied coolly. 'James doesn't need a—*dancer* for a wife.' She made the word sound like the ultimate insult.

'I think that should be James's decision,' Philippa retorted, her eyes blazing with hurt anger. 'But before we go any further, let's get a couple of things straight.

If my parents were alive, they might think that James wasn't good enough for *me*. A title and money and a magnificent house don't make him the perfect man! And here's something else for you to think about. You should appreciate James more, because he's certainly the best son you could have hoped for. He'll do absolutely anything to protect you and keep you well, even——'

She abruptly stopped, realising that she had been about to blurt out the real reason for their marriage—that James was determined to spare his mother the ordeal of a family scandal. Lady Haverford seemed startled by Philippa's outburst, but the sound of a Jeep skidding to an abrupt halt by the gate distracted her attention and halted her reply.

Philippa felt the last of the colour drain from her face as she saw James striding up the path. He stopped when he was just a few feet away and looked first at Philippa, his face grim and accusing, and then more gently at his mother.

'What's going on here?' he demanded. Then his gaze swung back to Philippa. 'What are you doing here?'

'I got lost,' she said, hating to hear the defensive note in her voice. She hadn't done anything *wrong*. 'I stopped to ask for directions.'

'Wait for me in the Jeep,' he ordered.

'But——'

'Wait in the Jeep, Philippa,' he repeated, and she didn't dare disobey him when he used that tone of voice.

She walked shakily back down the path while James took his mother back into the house. He was gone for some time, and she had managed to get just a little of her nerve back by the time he finally came out again.

He got into the Jeep but made no attempt to switch on the engine. Instead his gaze locked on to her face.

'I warned you not to upset my mother,' he reminded her in a hard voice.

'She upset *me*,' Philippa protested. Then she was horrified to feel the hot prickle of tears at the back of her eyes. Oh, no, she couldn't start to cry, she just couldn't!

Very hurriedly, she blinked hard. She wished James would stop staring at her like that. She didn't want him to see that her eyes were suspiciously bright.

'I didn't mean to come here,' she said rapidly. 'I didn't *know* this was your mother's house. If I had, I wouldn't have come near it! I certainly wish that I *had* stayed away,' she added, quickly rubbing her eyes with the back of her hand. 'Your mother is a dreadful snob. She said some horrible things to me!'

James just continued to look at her, until every one of her nerves felt stretched to its very limit by the intense gaze of those blue Haverford eyes. When he finally spoke, though, his voice was unexpectedly quiet.

'Of course my mother is a snob. It's the way she was brought up, in an age and background very different from ours. Rigid discipline and morals were drummed into her from an early age, and she was taught that certain classes of people don't mix, not in any circumstances. She's too old now to change; you simply have to accept that she lives very much in the past. And, believe it or not, she does have a nice side to her. She can be very generous and kind, when you get to know her.'

'But she doesn't want to get to know me,' Philippa reminded him. 'She thinks I'm definitely one of the lower classes. Not fit to lick the boots of any of the blue-blooded Haverfords! She doesn't like me, she doesn't approve of me, she doesn't want me within a hundred miles of Sherringborne!'

'Or of me,' James said drily. 'She's made that very clear.'

'I think she's very ungrateful,' Philippa burst out. 'After all, you're *doing* this for her!'

His face altered, became unreadable for a few moments. Then his mouth set into a controlled line. 'Yes, I am, aren't I?' he agreed in a flat tone. He switched on the engine, but instead of driving off he turned back to her. 'But she isn't ever to know that,' he warned. 'You do understand what the consequences will be, Philippa, if you ever tell her?'

She swallowed hard as she remembered how she had nearly blurted it out!

James's hand moved towards her and his fingers traced a light pattern under her chin as he held her face relentlessly towards him.

'Just remember the rules and everything will go very smoothly,' he told her in a voice that was suddenly low and velvet-soft. 'Stay away from my mother. Don't antagonise Stephanie. And accept that our marriage will only work if we both remember why we're entering into it.'

He drove swiftly back to the house, while his last words swirled round and round inside Philippa's head. Oh, yes, she remembered why they were getting married. He was doing it to avoid a scandal. And she was meant to be jumping at the chance of ensnaring a rich and titled husband! She wondered if she would ever dare tell him that she would marry him if he were completely penniless, homeless and out of work...

Philippa somehow got through the next few days without plunging into any major crises. James's self-control had very much slammed back into place, and they were almost unnaturally polite to each other when they were together. Stephanie still kept out of Philippa's way much of the time. Philippa rather regretted that because, despite the girl's behaviour, she would still have liked the chance to try and put things right between them, and make an effort to get to know her better. She realised that she was beginning to identify with Stephanie, because she knew only too well how the loss of both parents could knock your life completely off course. Although her own childhood had been so restricted, and she hadn't been at all happy at home, the death of her parents had still hit her so hard that it had taken her ages before she had even started to get over it. Thinking back to how it had affected her, remembering how she had behaved at the time, she began to understand why Stephanie was often so very abrasive. It seemed so important to make everyone think that you were dealing with your loss in a mature and intelligent manner, and the outward show of toughness was just a front to hide all the loneliness and insecurity locked away inside.

That was why, when Philippa walked into the drawing-room one afternoon and found Stephanie sitting on the sofa, reading a book, she ignored the hostile look that Stephanie immediately shot at her and sat down in the nearby armchair.

'Look,' she said bluntly, 'I know that you've made up your mind not to like me, but you could at least talk to me. It can get very lonely in this house, and there are times when I'd really like some company.'

'Lonely?' repeated Stephanie with a touch of curiosity, as if it had never occurred to her before that Philippa could have such feelings.

Encouraged by the fact that the girl hadn't actually been outright rude to her for once, Philippa looked at the book in her hand.

'Are you reading anything interesting?'

'Shakespeare,' Stephanie said, wrinkling her nose. 'It's for a school project.'

'Do you want to go on to university when you've finished school?'

'No,' she said at once. 'I'm going to be a model.' Then, seeing the look on Philippa's face, she added impatiently, 'Yes, I *know* that's what practically every girl my age says. But I mean it! I want to earn a lot of money very quickly, and I can do that as a top model.'

'You're only interested in the money?' Philippa said with growing curiosity.

'Yes.' Stephanie hesitated for a moment, then obviously decided that she might as well tell Philippa the rest of it. 'I want to buy a house just like Sherringborne Manor. And I'm going to need a lot of money for that.'

'You certainly are,' Philippa agreed. 'Why do you want a house just like this one?'

'Because I'm never going to own Sherringborne, of course.' Her face was bright and alive now; she was no longer the scowling, unattractive teenager that Philippa was used to seeing. All at once, Philippa could recognise the potential in this young girl; she could see the looks that were going to develop over the next couple of years. 'Even if Uncle James never marries and has children, I won't get the Manor,' Stephanie went on. 'It'll go to Jonathan. And I love this house; I always have. I want one *just* like it, one that will be mine forever and ever!'

Philippa was startled by the unexpected passion in Stephanie's voice. And at the same time she recognised the strength of will that lay beneath it. There was a great deal of James Haverford in his niece.

'If you really want to be a model, perhaps I could help,' Philippa offered. 'I've a friend who's in the business; she could probably give you some good advice on how to get started. And if you don't mind my being completely honest, I think you could do a lot to help yourself. If you want people to take your ambition seriously, you ought to do something about the way you look.'

Stephanie immediately bristled. 'The way I look is my business!'

'Of course it is,' Philippa agreed at once. 'But you're not making the most of yourself. You're already thirteen, Stephanie. Some girls your age are already doing part-time modelling. You need to start getting it together right now, or you might miss your chance.'

The belligerence slowly faded from Stephanie's face. 'OK, that makes sense,' she said slowly. 'What kind of things should I do?'

'I can only suggest the obvious. Get your hair cut at a really good hairdressers and get it into top condition. Make sure you eat plenty of fresh fruit and vegetables, and drink lots of water or fruit juice to keep your skin in good condition. Your height and weight are fine, but the way you move is almost as important. Perhaps you should think about taking dancing lessons. And if you want me to I'll get in touch with my friend. She'll be able to give you a lot of inside information, tell you how to put together a portfolio and give you the names of some of the best agencies to contact.' Philippa looked at Stephanie directly. 'Of course, you might not want my help. If you don't, just tell me straight away and I won't waste my time.'

But Stephanie was already looking at her with the glimmerings of a new respect. 'No, I really want to do this. I'll take help from anyone.'

'Even me?' Philippa said wryly.

Stephanie actually smiled. 'Even you,' she said, and her tone was almost friendly.

'Then I'll see what I can do. It would probably be best if you met up with my friend. I'll give her a ring during the next couple of days and try and fix up a meeting.'

'Thanks,' Stephanie said a little awkwardly, as if it was a word she wasn't used to saying very often. Then she picked up her book. 'I'd better go up to my room and make a start on this project. I don't think Uncle James will let me drop out of school to become a model!'

'No, I don't think he will,' Philippa said with a grin.

After Stephanie had left, Philippa picked up a magazine from the table, and she was about to flick idly through the pages when the door at the far end of the room opened.

As always, her nerves leapt to attention as James walked in. And when she saw his face her heart gave a heavy, irregular thud. She recognised that dark, fierce look in his eyes!

'I told you not to interfere in Stephanie's life,' he growled at her.

'You were eavesdropping,' she accused.

'I've the right to know what bad advice you're freely handing out to my niece.'

'It wasn't bad advice,' she argued hotly. 'She just needed some guidance and I tried to give it.'

James walked swiftly over until he was intimidatingly close. Philippa refused to give ground, though. Instead she stared defiantly back at him.

'Stephanie is just thirteen,' he reminded her in an edged tone. 'And she needs to give all her attention to her school work.'

'Of course she does,' Philippa agreed. 'But she's still old enough to start thinking about her career. And if she's serious about modelling, then this is the right time to get some facts and perhaps try and get some part-time work.'

'She is not going to be a model,' James stated bluntly.

'Don't you think that should be her own choice?' Philippa challenged him.

'I want her to go to university.'

'Of course you do. But if she isn't interested in academic subjects, then she's simply going to hate it. Anyway, Stephanie's very much a Haverford,' Philippa observed wryly. 'She's definitely got a mind of her own, and she intends to use it! Try and push her into something that she doesn't want to do and she'll simply rebel. She's very like you in a lot of ways,' she added rather recklessly. 'I bet that *you* never did what your parents wanted when you were younger.'

James stared at her for a few moments. 'You're right,' he said at last. 'I didn't. But that doesn't mean I approve of Stephanie's choice of career,' he added warningly.

'If she makes it to the top as a model, she'll have a very interesting life for a few years,' Philippa said persuasively. 'She'll travel, she'll meet and learn how to cope with a whole range of different people, and she'll earn very good money.' She hesitated, then added, 'I promised to put her in touch with a friend of mine who could give her advice.'

'I know,' said James in a disapproving tone. 'I heard.' He was silent again for a while. Then, to her amazement, he added, 'All right, let her talk to your friend. But don't interfere any more,' he warned.

Philippa gave a slightly impatient sigh. 'I can't help Stephanie, I mustn't talk to your mother—what *can* I do? I'm used to working. I'm getting very bored doing nothing all day.'

James's dark eyebrows shot up. 'I thought you'd jump at the chance to live in idle luxury,' he said with some of his old cynicism.

'Well, you're wrong,' she retorted. 'I want to do something that'll stretch my mind and keep me busy. Something useful.'

He walked over to the window and stood there for a couple of minutes, as if he needed time to think over her unexpected announcement. Philippa stared at the familiar breadth of his back. Today, because he had been working around the estate, he was dressed very casually in jeans and sweatshirt. She realised that she wanted to run her hand over the soft cotton, feel the hard, strong muscle and bone underneath. She had to clench her fist to keep her hand at her side.

He abruptly swung back to face her, making her jump slightly.

'All right,' he said in a businesslike tone. 'If you're serious, then there's no reason why our marriage shouldn't be a working partnership. I told you some time ago that the west wing of the house is used for business conferences and meetings. A great deal of organisation is required to make sure that everything runs smoothly and successfully. If you want to try something new, then why don't you take it over and try running it yourself?'

'Me?' she said in amazement. 'But I've never done anything like that. I wouldn't know where to start!'

He shrugged dismissively. 'Then forget it.'

'No,' Philippa said at once. She found that she wanted to prove to him that she could tackle something difficult and make a go of it. 'I want to try. Where do I start?'

'You're serious about this?' he challenged her. 'It'll mean a great deal of hard work and long hours.'

'I'm serious,' she said very firmly.

He looked at her with an unexpected glimmering of new respect. She liked that look; liked it a lot.

'Then we'll begin first thing in the morning,' he said. 'I'll take you around with me for the next couple of weeks, so you can learn exactly how the estate is run, and how the conference centre fits in. You can sit in on meetings, go through the books and meet everyone involved in the running of the estate. Things are relatively slack at the moment; it's the middle of summer and most people are away on holiday. It'll soon be autumn, though, and that's when the conference season begins again. By then you should have learnt enough to handle most of that side of the business.'

Philippa felt a surge of pure happiness. She was going to work beside James. Spend almost every hour of the day with him! She couldn't wait until tomorrow morning to begin.

She very soon discovered, though, that James was a relentlessly hard taskmaster. He was capable of hours of intense work without a break, and expected the same level of concentration from other people—including her. She had to work ferociously hard to keep up with him as she set about learning everything about Sherringborne.

She soon became very familiar with the day-to-day running of the estate and the functions of the various members of staff. James kept his promise and took her everywhere with him. She visited the farmers who worked on the estate, met the bankers, solicitors and accountants who dealt with the Haverford family's complex finances. She discovered that she had an unexpected aptitude for figures, a talent that she had never even known she possessed. In a very short time she could read a balance sheet as easily as a newspaper, and understood most of what was discussed at the meetings with the bankers and accountants.

She realised, with a sense of shock, that she was happy. Dangerously happy. And it was because she was spending so much time with James!

Philippa had seen quite a different side of him over the past couple of weeks. She watched and was fascinated by the skilful way he dealt with the people he employed, and quickly realised how much respect they had for him. She had known all along how important his family was to him, but she was beginning to realise just how much of his personal time and energy he gave to them. He dealt with his mother's complicated financial affairs as well as his own, and gave her advice whenever she needed it, and he was always ready to listen to Stephanie if she had a problem, or simply wanted to talk about something.

During all this time, though, he maintained a strictly working relationship with Philippa. His self-control was formidable and she saw him quickly curb the occasional unguarded gleam of desire in his eyes. She sometimes had to remind herself that he wasn't training her as his personal assistant, but as his prospective wife!

At the end of the following week, they had a late meal together one evening, just the two of them. They finished eating, and James raised his head and looked at her with some satisfaction.

'This arrangement seems to be working,' he said. 'The gossip has died down, and there's been no hint of scandal. Once the wedding is over, the problem should be resolved completely.'

'And that's all you've really wanted all along, isn't it?' she said slowly, some of her recent happiness beginning to fade away. Or perhaps it had never really been there in the first place—it had just been an illusion, something she had wanted so badly that she had imagined it.

He hesitated for just a moment. 'Of course,' he then said smoothly.

She pushed away her coffee. Suddenly, she couldn't drink it. The last couple of weeks had been wonderful, but almost dream-like. Perhaps it was time to face up to reality.

'And what about *our* problems?' she forced herself to say. 'It seems to me that they're just beginning.'

'There's no reason why we should have any problems,' he said crisply. 'We work together well—surprisingly well,' he added. 'And you enjoy the work, don't you?'

'Yes,' she said truthfully. 'Very much. But that wasn't what I meant. Look,' she said, the words suddenly spilling out of her, 'perhaps this is a good time to call the whole thing off. You said it yourself, the gossip and scandal have just faded away. We don't need to go through with this marriage.'

James's face instantly altered. So did his relaxed tone of voice. 'Oh, but we do,' he said much more grimly. 'I'm not having all this hard work undermined at the last moment. A broken engagement will give the story fresh impetus; it might encourage the Press to rake up all the old dirt. I won't have that. This marriage goes ahead.'

'What——?' She grabbed hold of the last of her courage, and forced herself to say, 'What if I won't let it?'

He got up and came to stand behind her.

'But you will, won't you, Philippa?' he said softly. He rested his hands on her shoulders for a few moments. Then his hands slid down over her breasts, outlining their small, firm shape, his palm pressing against the racing beat of her heart.

She wanted to say that she *wouldn't*, but she couldn't say anything at all. She closed her eyes, fought a losing battle against the tendrils of pleasure that were already curling through her body. This wasn't fair, she thought a little desperately. He knew what he was doing to her, and he wouldn't stop until he had undermined the very last of her resistance.

She was right. James's hands began to move with new determination. He was still standing behind her, still touching her only with his fingers and palms, but that was enough. While they had been working together over the last couple of weeks, he hadn't kissed her, had barely touched her, and she had *missed* it so much. All the old, hot longing now poured into her, burning its way right through her, and she couldn't force it back, didn't even want to try. As he opened her shirt, so that his palms could rest against her silky bare skin, she put her own hands over his and pressed them even harder against her, wanting to feel the fierce imprint of bone and muscle.

James slid one forefinger down the soft hollow between her breasts and gently caressed over and over, sending a cascade of delicious sensations right down into the pit of her stomach.

'You are going to marry me,' he ordered, his voice a little rough.

Philippa closed her eyes and simply surrendered. Her little show of token resistance was over. She had known right from the very beginning that she was frighteningly vulnerable where this man was concerned. One look from those brilliant blue eyes and her independence flew right out of the window. He had destroyed her fragile relationship with Jonathan, turned her life upside-down and her emotions inside out. What else was he going to do to her?

She shivered, but still had to say the words.

'Yes, I'm going to marry you,' she whispered, and shivered again as she realised that, very soon, she would be Philippa Haverford, Countess of Sherringborne.

Next morning, Philippa stood and stared out of the window for ages. All of this was going to be hers. The beautiful gardens, the magnificent house—and James. She still couldn't quite believe it, even though she knew that James was determined to go through with the marriage.

When she finally went downstairs, she found James waiting for her. Just the sight of him made her toes curl with sheer pleasure. And when he lightly touched her arm she could feel her skin instantly flush with heat.

'I've got a surprise for you,' he said, but there was a distinctly cool note in his voice, and Philippa had the feeling that this particular surprise didn't please him very much.

'What is it?' she asked.

'It's who it is,' he told her. Again, there was that restrained undertone, and she could sense a controlled tension in his muscles.

She shook her head. 'I don't understand——'

'He's waiting for you in the drawing-room.'

Philippa followed him as he began to walk swiftly in that direction. A puzzled look had settled over her face. What was this all about? And why was James in this rather odd mood?

As soon as she walked through the door to the drawing-room, though, her face cleared and she gave a huge grin.

'Jonathan! What on earth are you doing here? I thought you were on your way to Australia.'

Jonathan bounded over and gave her a huge hug. 'I felt so badly about the way I behaved that I had to fly back and see you first,' he said. 'I phoned earlier in the week, and Uncle James told me that you were still here.'

'He also wants to borrow some money to finance his trip to Australia,' James said drily.

Jonathan gave his bright, charming smile, the one that Philippa remembered so well. 'Just a temporary shortage of funds.' Then he turned back to Philippa. 'You look wonderful,' he said admiringly. 'I must have been mad to give you up.'

'And how is Nicky?' Philippa asked pointedly.

He had the grace to look rather sheepish. 'She's fine. I'm going to meet up with her in Hong Kong, then we're flying on together.' His gaze was still lingering on her. 'I'd forgotten how gorgeous you are,' he said a little wistfully. 'Sexy, but classy.'

'Jonathan,' she said warningly.

He grinned again. 'OK, sorry. I really do love Nicky, you know. But we did have a good time together while it lasted, didn't we?'

Philippa could see James's face rapidly darkening, and she wondered why. Her relationship with Jonathan had been fun and very innocent, and nothing had happened that James could possibly object to. And it was good that she and Jonathan were obviously going to remain good friends. James was beginning to behave as if he were *jealous* of his nephew, though. She knew that had to be completely impossible, but he was certainly looking fiercely furious about something!

Later on, they all had lunch together. James hardly said a word. Instead he sat opposite her and Jonathan with a brooding look on his face, watching the pair of them intently all through the meal. Philippa tried to chat brightly to Jonathan, but she could feel the laser-like intensity of James's blue gaze and she fidgeted uncomfortably and ate very little.

When lunch was over, James left to keep an important business appointment, and Jonathan announced that he was going to visit his grandmother. He invited Philippa to go with him, but she gave a wry grin and told him that she didn't think Lady Haverford would be very pleased to see her.

'Doesn't approve of the forthcoming nuptials to Uncle James?' he said perceptively. He had received the news with genuine delight and congratulations, which had been a great relief to Philippa.

'I think that if I were the last eligible woman left on earth, she *still* wouldn't want James to marry me,' Philippa said ruefully.

'Don't let it bother you,' he advised. 'You could have royal blood and a huge fortune, and Grandma still wouldn't think you were suitable. No one's ever been quite good enough for her blue-eyed son. She'll come round eventually—especially if you give her a batch of grandchildren!'

'We're not even married yet,' Philippa said, going bright red. At the same time, though, her heart began to thump away happily. She loved the idea of having James's children.

James's business appointment was in London, which meant he would be gone for several hours, so she had the afternoon to herself. When Jonathan came back from his grandmother's, he took Stephanie out for a slap-up tea, and the house seemed very quiet with no Haverfords in it.

Jonathan and Stephanie returned quite late. Philippa joined them for coffee, then Stephanie yawned hard a couple of times and decided to go up to bed.

After she had gone, Jonathan looked at Philippa with raised eyebrows. 'Still no Uncle James?'

'His business must have taken longer than he expected,' she said a little defensively.

'You'll have to keep a careful watch on him after you're married,' he teased, a wicked gleam appearing in his eyes. 'He's rather naughty where women are concerned.'

But Philippa was determined not to let Jonathan's thoughtless teasing upset her. 'He says the same thing about you,' she retorted. At the same time, though, her eyes darted involuntarily towards the doorway. Where *was* James?

She and Jonathan talked for a while longer. He told her more about his plans for travelling around the Far East and Australia, he showed her photos of Nicky, who was tousle-haired and beautiful in a tomboyish way, and then he too began to yawn.

'Time to hit the sack,' he said, getting to his feet. 'I'm off fairly early in the morning.'

'You're only staying one night?' Philippa said in surprise.

'I don't want to stay away from Nicky one day longer than I have to,' he admitted. 'And Uncle James came through with the funds, so I phoned the airport straight away and booked a flight.'

'I'll miss you,' she said with genuine affection.

'And I'll miss you,' Jonathan said, giving her hair a gentle tug. Then he gave her a quick, mischievous smile. 'How about a goodnight kiss, for old times' sake?'

'Just a *friendly* kiss,' Philippa said warningly.

'Of course. I promise.'

And he kept his promise. The kiss was light and warm, a brotherly kiss.

When it was over, Philippa looked up at him and smiled. 'That was nice.'

Before Jonathan could reply, James's voice cut in from the doorway.

'I'm glad that you liked it,' he said harshly. 'Why don't you do it again?'

Philippa's heart absolutely plummeted, and even Jonathan looked anxious as he turned to face his uncle.

'Don't get the wrong idea——' he began quickly.

'How could I?' James interrupted, that iron self-control cutting in again and keeping his voice grimly level. His blue gaze swept over them, his expression quite unreadable, and yet everything about him signalled danger. 'It was a kiss, that was all. Jonathan, don't you think that you should be in bed? It's late, and you've got to be up early to catch your flight.'

Jonathan took the hint very quickly, and hurried towards the door.

'Er—goodnight,' he said uncomfortably, pausing for just a moment in the doorway. Then he took another look at James's taut, darkening features, and rapidly disappeared.

James turned to face Philippa. She licked her dry lips as a wave of pure nervousness swept over her.

'I think we ought to talk about this,' she said a little shakily. 'You've obviously got the wrong idea——'

'I'm not interested in talking,' James cut in abruptly. 'And, from what I've seen tonight, nor are you. But we *are* both interested in kissing, aren't we?' he went on, his voice soft now, and yet subtly menacing. 'Although for very different reasons.'

'That was just a friendly kiss,' she said defensively.

'Perhaps it was. Perhaps it wasn't. I don't really care. But this kiss definitely isn't friendly,' James warned, his eyes glittering so brightly that they dazzled her.

He took two rapid strides towards her, then his mouth closed over hers with a fierce intensity that shook her to the very roots of her soul. He took her breath away; darkness began to swirl around her as his lips bruised hers harder and harder, as if he was absolutely determined to stamp the shape of his mouth on hers forever.

When he finally released her, Philippa's knees sagged weakly. She didn't think that she could cope with a kiss like that too often! But it was over now, and she had survived.

Then she looked into James's dark, powerful face and realised that it wasn't over at all. It was only just beginning!

'Time to make an important decision,' James said, his eyes locking on to hers with an intensity that made her begin to tremble wildly. 'Either you belong to me or you don't. Which is it, Philippa?'

'I belong to you,' she whispered almost inaudibly.

'Do you?' There was a note of utter cynicism in his voice. 'I don't think so.'

'Because I kissed Jonathan goodnight?' she said incredulously.

'And what else would you like to do with Jonathan?' he challenged her, his body completely rigid with angry tension.

'What on earth are you talking about?'

'Don't play the innocent,' James ordered, his voice hard. 'You understand very well what I mean. But let's get one thing straight right now. You can't have both of us.'

'I don't *want* both of you,' she said, beginning to get very angry at his accusations. He had absolutely no right to say these things to her, behave like this!

'I think that you do,' James said harshly. 'I think that you're a girl who's greedy enough to want it all. A rich, titled husband *and* a young lover!'

Philippa felt as if he had physically slapped her. And the shock of his words had a profound effect on her. She forgot the dizzy pleasure of his kisses and caresses; she stared at his mouth and didn't even see its rigidly beautiful outline. With a gut-wrenchingly painful jerk, she had finally been brought to her senses.

She realised that she had agreed to marry a man who not only didn't love her, but didn't even trust her. She felt as if she had been a little crazy these last few weeks, but now she was perfectly sane—even though she was hurting like hell.

'You're wrong,' she said in a flat and empty voice, looking at him now as if he were a total stranger. 'I never wanted it all. And I've just decided that I don't want *any* of it. Not ever!'

'What the hell are you talking about?' James demanded.

She didn't even answer him. Instead she turned round and walked away from him. She had been afraid that he would come straight after her, but he seemed frozen into immobility. Or perhaps he just didn't care enough to try and stop her leaving, she thought bitterly.

Philippa went up to her room, quickly packed, and then went back downstairs. She knew that she had to leave now, before all the old feelings for James began to surge back and forced her to change her mind. The house was utterly silent and very dark. No sign of James. No rigidly angry face looming out of the shadows, no hand clamping around her arm, preventing her from leaving.

She swung open the heavy front door and walked out into the warm, velvet black night.

She felt so very alone, but there was nothing new about that. What was new was the pain that was tying all her nerve-ends into knots. But she would get over that, she told herself. She *would* get over it.

Philippa kept on walking into the darkness, until Sherringborne Manor—and its arrogant, angry, impossible owner—was left far behind.

CHAPTER NINE

PHILIPPA wearily pulled on her spangled costume. Just one more routine to get through and then the show would be over for another night. Only that wasn't really a relief, because it meant that it would be time for her to return to her empty, lonely lodgings.

It was nearly two weeks since she had left Sherringborne. For the first week, she had stayed in her flat and nearly gone quietly mad. It had been one of her friends who had bluntly told her to get back to work, before she cracked up completely.

Another friend had used his contacts in the business to help her get this job. It was in a summer show, at a resort on the south coast. One of the girls in the chorus line had gone sick and Philippa was temporarily standing in for her. She had been lucky enough to find a room to rent locally for the couple of weeks she would be here, and she knew that getting involved in the show, the sheer hard work involved in learning the new routines in such a very short time, had pulled her back to some kind of sanity.

Looking back, she couldn't believe that she had ever agreed to marry James in the first place. Someone who didn't love her, who was just ruthlessly using her to protect his mother's health and his family name from scandal. That really *had* been madness!

Sherringborne must have cast a spell over her, she told herself more than once. She had behaved irrationally all the time she had been there, done things that she would normally never have dreamt of doing.

Every morning when she woke up she resolutely told herself that she wouldn't think of James today. She wouldn't wonder what he was doing, where he was going, whom he was with. Whether he had even given her a single thought after she had walked out on him that night. She never succeeded, of course, but she stubbornly kept on fighting her obsession.

The music began, and the other girls in the dressing-room began to surge back towards the stage. Philippa followed them, still tugging her costume into place. They had a vigorous dance routine to get through before the star of the show, a well-known comic, stepped into the spotlight and went into his main act.

As usual, the audience was a dark blur beyond the bright lights that blazed down on the stage. Halfway through the routine, though, Philippa became aware of a stir of movement in one of the aisles. She could see a couple of the other girls glancing in that direction as they went through their athletic dance number, and then Philippa could actually see a dark figure leaping up the steps at the far end of the stage.

The steps had been put there so that the comic could go down into the audience and involve some of the people in the front rows in his act. They certainly weren't meant to be used by a member of the audience trying to get on to the stage!

Philippa gave a small shrug and danced on. She supposed someone backstage would notice what was happening and take care of it. There were a couple of broad-shouldered stage hands who usually handled any trouble.

Then the man stepped on to the stage itself and Philippa suddenly nearly stopped breathing. It wasn't some rather drunk holiday-maker who thought it would be fun to join in the show. It was James!

She stood dead still, while the other girls danced on around her. No! she thought wildly. This just couldn't be happening!

James strode over to her and glared at her. 'I've come to get you,' he announced, his eyes boring into hers.

'Go *away*,' she said almost incoherently, her voice shaking as badly as her legs. 'You can't do this! I'll get the sack!'

'I don't give a damn about that.' He seized hold of her wrist. 'You're coming with me.'

She could hear the manager shouting at her from the wings, the other girls were staring in amazement while they tried to keep the dance routine going, and there was an increasing buzz from the audience as they tried to work out what was happening.

James began to drag her off the stage.

'Let go of me!' Philippa pleaded.

'No,' he said grimly, and his grip on her tightened.

When they reached the wings, the manager was standing there, his face red with fury.

'You're fired,' he shouted at her.

James gripped the man's lapels. 'Don't raise your voice at her,' he warned. 'I don't like it. And you haven't fired her. She's just quit.'

He didn't give her a chance to return to the dressing-room for her clothes. Instead, still wearing the brief, spangled costume, Philippa found herself hauled out into the car park and then bundled into a car.

James got in beside her.

'You can't do this!' she almost wept. 'All I had was this job, and now I haven't even got that.'

He ignored her. Instead he started the engine and drove off very swiftly.

Philippa started to fumble with the handle. 'Let me out,' she demanded, beginning to recover just a little from the sheer shock of what had happened.

'Don't touch that door,' James ordered, and he increased the car's speed.

Philippa had enough sense to realise that opening the door would be sheer suicide while they were travelling at this speed. Instead she turned and looked hotly at James.

'Where are you taking me?'

'To Sherringborne, of course.'

'I don't want to go there!'

'You're not being given a choice.'

The car swept on through the night, and she huddled down in the seat and tried to make some sense of all this. It was impossible, though. She didn't know why she was here. Why James looked so grim-faced and yet utterly determined.

At the speed they were travelling, it didn't take long to reach Sherringborne. The car hurtled up the wide drive, past the great trees that studded the sweep of grass on either side, and then skidded to a halt in front of the house.

James got out, strode round to her side of the car, opened the door and pulled her out. Philippa dug her heels in stubbornly.

'I'm not going inside,' she warned.

'Oh, yes, you are,' he said forcefully, then his hand was back round her arm again, levering her forward.

Philippa didn't want to get involved in a humiliating struggle with him on the drive. She would wait until she was inside the house, she told herself. Someone else was bound to be around, and he wouldn't dare behave like this in front of a member of staff or one of his own family.

But she had forgotten just how large Sherringborne was. And how very empty and silent it could seem, late at night. There was no one in the Great Hall. No one she could shout to for help as James steered her up the stairs at a speed that left her quite breathless.

And then, somehow, she was standing inside a large bedroom—and he was closing the door behind them!

That was when Philippa really began to panic. 'Let me out,' she said, her eyes huge with alarm. 'Let me out! *Right now*.'

But James stood there, the powerful set of his body completely blocking the doorway. She realised that he was wearing a dinner-jacket and pristine white shirt, as if he had come to the theatre straight from a very formal evening.

He stared at her own costume, brief and covered with rather gaudy sequins and glass jewels.

'As usual, we're a mismatched couple,' he growled. 'At least, in the eyes of the world.'

This close, Philippa could see the dark gleam in the depths of his brilliant blue gaze; she could feel the heat already radiating from his body.

'No,' she said at once. '*No*. You're not to do this to me. Not again.'

'When you say that and mean it, I'll let you go,' James promised.

She licked her lips with sudden nervousness. Yes, she could say it and mean it. She could!

James was perfectly still now, not a single muscle moving. She could hear the alteration in his breathing, though; it was quickening and becoming more irregular.

Probably no one else would have noticed it, but Philippa did. She suddenly knew that she was always going to notice absolutely everything about this man.

'Why don't you touch me?' he suggested softly. 'You know that you want to.'

She badly wanted to lie, to tell him that she certainly didn't. But her mouth simply wouldn't say the words. Instead she was horrified to find her hands obediently creeping towards him; they were actually touching the fine material of his shirt now, sliding the buttons free so that her fingertips—just her fingertips—could touch the hot, supple skin underneath.

Philippa couldn't believe that she was doing this. Not after everything he had done, all the torment of the last couple of weeks. And his behaviour tonight was quite unforgivable, hauling her off that stage in front of all those people, bringing her back here totally against her will.

Well, almost totally, she admitted. If she had fought harder, shouted louder, he would have been forced to let her go.

With some shame, she realised that a small part of her had simply gone along with this. And now she wanted to go still further. She wanted to let him do exactly what he wanted with her.

'Ready to admit it yet, Philippa?' James murmured, reading her thoughts with such disturbing ease that the colour instantly surged into her face. 'We want each other.' He gripped her wrists, held her hand close against him so that she could feel his swiftly contracting muscles beneath her palm. 'Do you know where I was tonight?' he went on. 'At a very formal reception, where I was meant to be giving an after-dinner speech. Halfway through the meal, I walked out. I knew where you were.

I've known where to find you every single day since you left here. And tonight I couldn't wait any longer.'

He slid her hand lower; she could feel the intimate beat of him against her fingers and it was almost like touching his soul, such a very private and intimate part of him. Philippa closed her eyes and knew that soon, very soon, she was going to be completely lost.

She felt him shudder deeply against her, as if he wanted this to end right now, locked against the softness of her cupped hand. At the very last moment he pulled away from her and held her at arm's length as the breath rasped hoarsely in his chest.

'We're both here tonight against our will. But neither of us is leaving until this is finally over,' he said in a thick voice. His breathing eased just a fraction, but the burning light never left his eyes. 'From now until morning there are no rules, no recriminations, no restrictions.'

In one swift movement he swept her off the ground. Then Philippa found herself being carried over to the bed.

Her glittering costume was removed with ruthless efficiency, with long, dark kisses to distract her as his hands released the frustratingly tiny catches that were difficult to unfasten. Every inch of her was explored with mind-bending pleasure as his mouth and hands roved over the soft curves of breast and stomach. He turned her over on to her stomach and let his fingers lightly massage the tight muscles of her shoulders until they were loose and relaxed. Then his hands moved slowly, slowly down the long line of her spine, sending long, deep shivers of pleasure right through every nerve-end in her body.

She began to throb inside and she was hot, so hot. He turned her back again, to face him, and this time his kisses were fiercely demanding. His fingers slid between her legs and the heat exploded into pleasure; she heard her own voice say something quite incoherently and knew that she was trying to beg for more.

'Do you still want to leave?' James demanded hoarsely.

She couldn't speak; she just shook her head blindly.

His fingers continued to caress until her body was sweat-soaked with pleasure and writhing restlessly under his touch. Her lips longed to kiss him again and he knew it; his mouth hovered over hers, tantalisingly close, making her wait and wait for the taste and warmth and fierce pressure. Then, when the kiss finally came, blindingly intense, he wouldn't release her until every last ounce of breath had sighed from her lungs.

His body burned against hers, hot and frustrated. He was still fully clothed, as if he needed to keep a barrier against her to stop himself simply taking her.

He wrenched off his jacket and tie. Then he turned back to her.

'You do the rest,' he invited throatily.

Philippa didn't hesitate. Her shaking fingers slid the shirt from his shoulders, and she found herself leaving a butterfly-light trail of kisses across the powerful spread of his chest. Then she bent her head, let her face rest against him so that she could feel the heavy thudding of his heart against her cheek. She turned her head further, and her mouth gently closed over the nearest nipple, her tongue softly caressing its roughened surface.

James's reaction was instant. Every muscle in his body briefly clenched into a rigid spasm and he abruptly pulled away from her.

'Who taught you to do that?' he demanded harshly.

She met his brilliant gaze without flinching. 'No one,' she said softly. 'It was just something that I wanted to do.'

He growled almost angrily, as if he didn't believe her. Then he shivered deeply as she slid her hands around his back, running her fingers over the strong outline of his shoulders.

'Enough,' he ordered, as if he was determined to put an end to this weakening of his self-control.

He removed the rest of his clothes himself, and when he turned back to her there was a hot glitter in his eyes.

'Which one of us will surrender first?' he murmured challengingly. 'I think that it'll be you, Philippa.'

Almost before he had finished saying her name, he had begun a relentless assault on her body, pushing her further and further down into a darkening, spinning pool of pleasure. Soft trails of kisses spun threads of fire from her breasts to her thighs, and as his dark head pressed lower his mouth found all the most vulnerable hollows and folds and sucked gently at their hot moistness. Philippa couldn't breathe, couldn't move, couldn't do anything as she ached and burned under his touch.

But James was also pushing himself too far; his body throbbed against hers with fresh urgency and with a sudden gasp of breath he slid inside her, as if he was powerless to hold back any longer.

Philippa was paralysed by the new sensations that flooded through her, drowning out absolutely everything except the sudden and frantic desire to press closer, still closer; she wanted this to end right now because she wasn't sure that she could stand it any longer.

But James fought back the pleasure; he kept rigidly still for a few moments and then forced her to move slowly, oh, so slowly, so that the fierce spasms inside her built with agonising intensity. She clung to him like a child who was lost, in desperate need of help. His own breathing was completely out of control now, but he somehow found enough will-power to compel his body to keep pace with hers instead of simply rushing to find its own frenzied pleasure. Each deep thrust was deliberately timed to match the involuntary shudders that ran through her, and she wasn't so naïve that she didn't know what it must be costing him to hold back, hold back, as her own, more inexperienced body strained for its own pinnacle of ecstasy.

But then it finally came, rushing through her with a force that absolutely stunned her, making everything that had gone before seem almost insignificant. James's own heated desire surged into her and someone seemed to be gasping his name—was it her? She didn't know; she was totally incapable of any kind of thought as the pleasure just ate her up.

It seemed to take forever for the world to return to any kind of sanity. Her body ached in the most delicious way and she was intensely aware of the impressive length of James's body lying beside her, still hot and damp with sweat, touching her intimately as he curled round her possessively.

'Do you like this game that we've just played?' he murmured in her ear.

Philippa stiffened a fraction. Game? Had this really been just a game to him? Dragging her off that stage, bringing her back here—had it all been just for his *amusement*?

A little of the magic began to slide away and she couldn't seem to get it back again. James's hand moved against her in a relaxed way, obviously still interested in her despite everything that had just happened between them, and she desperately wanted to respond, but she couldn't.

He sensed her tenseness. 'What is it?'

'Nothing,' she mumbled.

James's forefinger gently stroked the soft underside of her breast, and she actually drew back from him.

Even without looking at him, she knew that a dark frown was gathering on his face.

'Don't do this,' he ordered.

'What am I meant to do?' she said unhappily. 'Pretend that this has somehow made everything all right? But it hasn't. It can't!'

He raised himself up on one elbow and began to look a little fierce.

'Don't spoil this, Philippa,' he warned.

'Spoil what?' she said, fighting to keep the tears from her eyes. 'There's nothing *to* spoil. You wanted me and I wanted you. That's it, isn't it? Nothing more!' At least, not on his side. She sat up jerkily and began to fumble a little frantically for her clothes. 'I've got to go,' she said.

'What the hell are you talking about?' he demanded sharply. 'Go where?'

'I don't know.' Oh, damn, she didn't have any clothes. Just that stupid costume. There was a bathrobe at the foot of the bed and she dragged it on. It was too big—it must belong to James; it held the fresh scent of his body, and unhappiness rolled through her again like a huge wave that was threatening to drown her. 'I've just got to get away from here.'

His eyes darkened. 'Don't you dare pretend that you didn't enjoy what just happened between us!'

'I'm not pretending anything,' she said a little desperately. 'But there isn't anything *more*, is there? At least, not for you.'

'What the hell are you talking about?'

'I suppose I might as well tell you. It doesn't really matter any more. You see, I love you,' Philippa blurted out. 'I always have. That's why I agreed to marry you. Why I went along with the whole charade. I knew that you didn't love me but I was so stupid, I thought that I could live with that, as long as I could be with you. But I can't. I know that now. So it's best to leave straight away, because it would be so stupid to go on hoping that everything will miraculously turn out all right when it won't, it can't.'

She had pulled the bathrobe on by now with shaking hands, and she was backing towards the door as she talked. Her heart hammered away at breakneck speed as James levered himself off the bed and began to move towards her, tall, powerful, authoritative. She stared at his naked body hungrily for an instant, then lifted her gaze to his fierce and angry blue eyes. Despairingly, she wondered how she was going to get through the rest of her life without him. But she had to try. What was the alternative? A few nights in his bed, whenever he decided that he wanted her? That would be hell on earth!

'Just let me go,' she pleaded softly as he finally stopped just a few feet away.

'You're not walking out on me!'

'I'm sorry if that hurts your pride. I don't want to do *anything* that hurts you. But I'm going, I've just got to——'

She wrenched open the door and ran through it. He lunged towards her, but she was too quick for him, and she was hurtling down the stairs in just seconds.

Philippa thought at first that he wasn't going to come after her. But he must have paused just to grab a robe for himself, because by the time she reached the foot of the stairs she could hear his bare feet pounding on the oak treads.

She began to run, without even thinking where she was going. Along the corridor, through the entrance to the Great Hall, hardly able to see in the darkness. She crashed into one of the solid oak chairs with such force that she sent it flying. She didn't even feel the bruises; she darted on to the heavy door of the main entrance, grabbing the massive handle and trying to open it.

It was locked. Philippa pounded on it in sheer frustration, and tears poured down her face as she realised she was trapped. She turned round, totally defeated, to find James confronting her.

'No,' she cried. '*No*. Go away!'

He seized hold of her wrists. 'That wasn't what you said to me earlier,' he said angrily. He freed one of his hands and flicked down the light switch next to the door. Then he stared at her face and his blue eyes suddenly looked tormented. 'Don't cry,' he ordered. '*Don't cry*. I can't stand it!'

'Then let me leave,' she sobbed.

'No,' he said implacably. 'You're going to stay here. And you're going to marry me.'

'Don't say that. That charade is over! There's never going to be any marriage between us. You don't even want it. You never wanted it.'

'Don't tell me what I want,' James said in a very strained voice. 'And since you've told me that you love me, that seems a very good reason for you to stay and marry me.'

But Philippa shook her head almost violently. 'I never meant to say that. I didn't want you to know. But since this seems to be the night for telling the truth, I'll admit something else. Tonight was wonderful—at least, it was for me. But it's finally made me face up to something that I didn't want to see before. I don't want sex without love, not even with you.'

'Nor do I,' James said tautly. His face had gone quite ashen while she had been speaking. 'You've learnt something tonight, but so have I. Something that I knew a long time ago, but absolutely refused to admit. You know that I wanted you almost from the moment I first saw you,' he said with complete frankness. 'Even before Jonathan wrote that letter and broke up your relationship, I couldn't keep my hands off you. I was angry with myself, I *despised* myself, but I couldn't stop touching you, kissing you. I wanted you in my bed,' he admitted freely. 'But the real shock came when I realised just how much more I wanted. I liked your independence, the way that you stood up to all of us. I know how intimidating the Haverfords can be, but you didn't let us browbeat you. I soon discovered there was a sharp brain inside that beautiful head, and that was intriguing as well. I wondered what you would be capable of achieving if you really set your mind to something. And then you gave good advice and help to Stephanie when she needed it. All right, so I didn't appreciate it at the time. But when I had time to think it over I realised that you really did want to give her sensible and sympathetic guidance. To put it bluntly, you had a hell of a lot of qualities that I admired.'

'I suppose it's nice to be admired,' Philippa said in a dull voice.

James suddenly shook her impatiently. 'Why aren't you listening to what I'm saying to you?'

'I am listening,' she insisted.

'No, you're not. Because otherwise you'd have heard what I was really saying.'

'Really saying?' she repeated in a confused tone.

'That it was easier to tell myself that I admired you rather than admit that I loved you! That I'd fallen in love with you almost from the first moment I saw you.' He ran his fingers through his hair in sudden exasperation. 'In the beginning, I kept telling myself that you were a fortune-hunter, the kind of woman I despised. And on top of that you already belonged to Jonathan. None of that made any difference, though. I still wanted you for myself. That made me angry. I'd never lost control of my emotions like that before, and I didn't like it. But I couldn't do anything about it. I still can't,' he admitted frankly. 'You can drive me mad by just looking at me with those big brown eyes. And when you touch me it's hard to stop myself going completely crazy.'

'You're—you're saying that you *love* me?' Philippa said in a totally disbelieving voice. Then she shook her head with sudden determination. 'You don't mean it. I know that you don't.'

'Why would I lie about it?' he demanded.

'I—don't know.'

James gave her another shake, as if she was driving him mad with frustration at her refusal to believe him. 'Do you know why I behaved the way I did that night I saw you kissing Jonathan?' he said, with a quick, fierce gleam in his eyes that made every bone in her body feel as if it had just melted clean away. 'I was so jealous that

I was almost out of my mind; I couldn't control what I said or did. I wanted to kill Jonathan. My own nephew!'

Philippa gave a loud gulp. 'It was just a friendly kiss.'

'I don't give a damn what kind of kiss it was. I don't want anyone touching your mouth but me. Not ever!' His grip on her arms tightened. 'When you ran out on me that night, I told myself, Fine, let her go, you don't need her, you can live without her. But I can't,' he said, his eyes flashing as if even now he hated having to make that admission. 'I held out for a couple of weeks, but then I just cracked. Halfway through one of the most important business dinners of the year tonight, I just got up and walked out. I knew where you were and I knew that I had to come and get you.'

'Even if it meant dragging me off stage in front of hundreds of people,' she reminded him with the first glimmerings of a very shaky smile.

'I wouldn't have cared if you'd been on network television and the whole country had been watching,' James growled. Then his gaze fixed on her face and suddenly darkened as he saw a fresh wave of uncertainty wash over it. 'Do you believe everything I've told you?' he demanded.

'Yes,' she said, but even she could hear the lack of conviction in her voice. It was so hard to accept that he was telling her the truth. She certainly wanted to believe it—she had never wanted anything more in her life!—but——

A familiar voice suddenly spoke to them from the far side of the Great Hall, making both of them spin round.

'Oh, for heaven's sake, Uncle James, just kiss her and tell her that you love her,' said Jonathan in exasperation. 'I thought that you knew all about women? Philippa wants to hear the words!'

Philippa stared at him. 'Jonathan? But—why aren't you in Australia?'

'It's a flying visit with Nicky,' he told her.

James glowered at his nephew. 'You're supposed to be in bed.'

'The two of you woke up, chasing each other round the house and then shouting at each other.'

Philippa went bright red and James continued to glare at Jonathan. 'Go back to your room,' he ordered, as if Jonathan were about six years old.

Jonathan merely grinned. 'Yes, Uncle James. But don't forget the advice I gave you.' Then he winked at Philippa, and left.

Philippa looked at James apprehensively. 'What—what are you going to do now?'

'What the hell do you think I'm going to do?' he groaned back at her, his eyes quite brilliant. 'I'm going to kiss you and tell you that I love you!'

Her eyebrows shot up. 'You mean you're actually going to take advice from your nephew?'

'I'll probably disinherit him in the morning,' James warned. 'But right now I'm willing to try anything that will force the truth inside that stubborn, beautiful head of yours.'

'It could take a long time,' she warned.

'I hope it does. In fact, I hope it takes all night.'

'Oh, so do I!' she said fervently. Then she closed her eyes in blissful anticipation as James's mouth swooped towards hers with utter determination. And just before his lips touched hers she heard the soft murmur of his voice. 'I love you.'

* * *

Philippa stood just inside the entrance of the packed church, with Jonathan beside her. He was going to give her away—an unconventional arrangement, but she was glad to have his familiar, friendly face beside her. And Stephanie was her bridesmaid, looking startlingly pretty in a dress of soft lilac silk.

A lot of the faces in the church were already familiar: people employed on the estate, local neighbours, the household staff. Philippa could see Braddock, the butler, still looking at her disapprovingly. She didn't care that he thought she was totally the wrong person to become the next Countess of Sherringborne. *She* knew that she was going to make a success of it.

There were plenty of Philippa's own friends, including Julie, who had flown over from Tunisia, and Mrs Mackie, her old neighbour, had been determined to come to Philippa's wedding.

In the front pew was Lady Haverford. Philippa gave a rueful smile. *Another* disapproving face. But James's mother was no longer openly hostile, apparently resigned to the unwelcome fact that her son had every intention of marrying this unsuitable girl, and remaining married to her for the rest of his life. And Philippa had the feeling that relations between them would improve still further when Lady Haverford was presented with her first grandchild.

Then Philippa saw James, waiting impatiently for her. Tall, dark, immaculately dressed, his vivid blue eyes alight with a mixture of love and desire—and he was hers! She certainly believed now that he loved her. In the few weeks leading up to the wedding he had made her believe it in a hundred different ways!

The music began to play, and she wanted to rush down the aisle and fling herself straight into his arms.

Better not! she warned herself with a quick grin. Lady Haverford would have a fit.

Instead she made herself walk sedately towards James, comforting herself with the thought that she could run into his arms every night for the rest of her life. And be welcomed by his possessive mouth, his hard body, and his love.

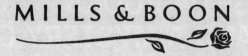